BARGAIN WITH FATE

SAGE:
BOOK TWO

Books and stories by Marian Allen

Novels

Eel's Reverence

Force of Habit

SAGE Book 1: The Fall of Onagros

SAGE Book 2: Bargain With Fate

SAGE Book 3: Silver and Iron

Sideshow in the Center Ring

Short Story Collections

Lonnie, Me and the Hound of Hell

Turtle Feathers

The King of Cherokee Creek

MA's Monthly Hot Flashes: 2002-2009

Visit the author at

http://MarianAllen.com

bargain with fate

sage:
book two

A Novel
by

marian allen

Per Bastet

Bargain With Fate Sage: Book Two

Second Edition

Copyright © 2014 Marian Allen

Published by Per Bastet Publications LLC, P.O. Box 3023 Corydon, IN 47112

Cover design by T. Lee Harris

ISBN 978-1-942166-52-8

DEDICATION:

To T. Lee Harris, without whom almost nothing would get done. Ever.

BARGAIN WITH FATE

SAGE:
BOOK TWO

PROLOGUE

Tortoise crawled onto the beach. He pushed himself along the damp sand parallel to the sea, his head swiveling from side to side. He stopped, having found what he had been looking for: a large, unbroken shell shaped like a shallow bowl.

He lifted his head and hissed.

Unicorn peered down from the moor above. With a series of seemingly careless leaps, she descended the rocky cliffs and joined him.

From the south, Dragon flew across the water.

Phoenix arrived from nowhere in a burst of light.

When they were gathered, Tortoise lowered his head and shed a tear into the empty shell.

The others were unmoved by his apparent sorrow.

"Oh, my brother," he said, in a voice so thick with grief no one could believe it sincere. "Oh, my sisters."

Dragon breathed a clear flame. Tortoise's false tear evaporated, leaving behind a slight residue of salt and hypocrisy.

Phoenix shook his head, yet it was he who said, "What are we to imagine you regret, my brother?"

"Why, the loss of His Grace's lovely young bride," said Tortoise. "Has she not disappeared? Is she not dead?" He cocked his head at Unicorn and, if he had had eyebrows, he would have cocked one. "She is dead, isn't she?"

Unicorn met his impertinent red gaze. "What does it matter?"

"Does it not matter that His Grace ordered the deaths of a host of children, on the chance that one of them might claim the throne? Does it not matter that His Grace's mother has ordered the capture and slaughter of *you*, my sister?"

Still, Unicorn met his gaze. "It's all one."

"To you, perhaps." Tortoise scraped at the sand in irritation. "Perhaps other people don't bear suffering so easily."

"I never said it was easy."

Tortoise turned to Dragon. "I know *you* agree with me, Sister."

"If I did," she said, "you would change your position."

Phoenix laughed bitterly and fluttered his wings, fanning his own flames and stretching his head upward, as if he longed to fly somewhere he couldn't reach.

Tortoise said, "Am I the only one who takes any interest in the lives of these poor mortals?"

Unicorn snorted and said, "Pity the poor mortal who interests you! Let them be!"

"Am I yours to command?"

"You are neither mine to command nor to fear. You are only to be endured. And, for a creature so slow, you seem to have reached the end of my patience with astounding swiftness." She picked her way back up the slope and vanished.

Dragon and Phoenix rose into the sky and performed an arabesque, Phoenix's fire glittering off Dragon's scales, then Dragon vanished into mist and Phoenix into haze.

Tortoise, left alone, stepped on the edge of the bowl-like shell, upending it. Grumbling all the way, he slipped back into the sea.

ChAPTER 1
A TRAP SET FOR VIRTUE

Rhu beren Robia lay in bed in the small hours after Elsie's disappearance, unable to sleep. His mind and spirit roiled in a muddle of clarities like water at the foot of a cataract: turbulent, but full of light and air. Elsie was gone, perhaps out of his life forever – but she was free, her body no longer a hostage to Sarpa's lineage.

Or was she free? Had she escaped, or had she been shunted into a captivity so close only the Kinninger knew of it? Or only the Kinninger's mother? Or had she been snatched, like a chestnut, from the fire, only to be consumed by her liberator?

Yet Rhu's qualms were only grains of sand, themselves glittering, in the roll and spray of his happiness. He felt – and knew that this was because he wanted to feel it, yet trusted the feeling as true – that Elsie was free.

If he, too, were free, he would find her. He would roam the world over and find her and take her or win her and have her for himself.

But he was not free. He was the Kinninger's man, and Layounna's man, and he could desert neither his lord nor his duty to search for his heart.

As day followed day, Rhu found confirmation of his hope. The conspiratorial amusement with which Landry spoke of the bridal fiction they maintained told Rhu that Landry, at least, had no deeper secret involving Elsie.

Those days also saw overtures of courtesy by Guthrie beren Melanell toward the Chamberlain. It pleased Rhu to think that Guthrie's rise in influence had reached its natural level and was now beginning to require maintenance. He could tolerate the Chief Sword's being made his social superior if it were plain, especially to Guthrie, that this position was artificial and insecure.

Oliva, too, seemed to court the Chamberlain's good will. She suddenly embellished her orders with smiles and fragile gestures. She reminisced about events from Rhu's boyhood (memorable to her when these were involved with episodes in her own past). She stood closer than had been her wont, and blinked her eyes as if they were growing weak, and fingered her silver hair.

Rhu would find himself responding with a strong retainer's gallantry toward his old mistress's failing powers. He would determine to meet the weakness of her decline with compassion, although she had met that of his youth with uncompromising coldness.

Then he would see that tuck at the corners of her mouth, that slight sluing of the eyes, that head-tilt that he knew from his earliest days. It meant she was working to control something or someone and was happy with her progress. Rhu didn't know whether to be repelled or flattered to find himself the object of that look.

Perhaps, he told himself, Landry was planning to give his Chamberlain an even greater part in governance. Co-regent was too much to think of, but was Deputy Regent?

Rhu judged it best to show no sign of his expectation, lest he seem presumptuous, and so deflect Landry's favor.

Then came the day when Oliva approached him with a quest.

"But how am I to make the capture?" Rhu was more bemused than anyone at his selection.

"The last reported sighting was in the Fiddlewood at its southern tip, on the border of the East and Central Districts. Don't ride into the Fiddlewood like a conqueror or creep about like a hunter, or you'll never glimpse your prey. If you go in on foot and walk without stealth, the unicorn won't avoid you. It may even seek you out. You'll be able to come close to it – close enough to touch it. Then you can put a halter on it and slip a steel bit into its mouth. It will be unable to free itself of the steel; the metal will scorch its mouth, and struggle will only increase the pain. Lead it out of the woods at dusk and bring it here as quickly as your horse will gallop. That will so weary it that we can bind it easily and carry it down into the temple."

"My Lady….," Rhu began, but ended by bowing.

"Tarkastrus tells me that the time will be most propitious at the new moon. Can you be ready by then?"

"I'm ready now. I'll leave tomorrow and search through the most propitious time, until the moon is full. If I haven't found any sign of the beast by then, there is no longer such a beast."

~*~

Rhu's horse, Ebenos, was black and looked less tall and muscular than he really was, under the body of his master. He was used to travel, but he was not used to his master's being uncertain in the saddle.

The Chamberlain told himself he welcomed this quest. It was the chance he needed to prove himself to Landry as a man of action. Oliva had made it clear that bringing back a unicorn would render the greatest possible service to the crown.

It was a chance, too, to go afield on his own. Maybe he'd find some sign of Elsie. If he did find such a sign, he had given himself a little time to follow it.

Suppose he found her – what then? Would the Kinninger thank him if he brought her back? And what would happen to Elsie, once recaptured?

Rhu thought, then, of the unicorn, exhausting itself in flight, vainly attempting to lessen the pain of base metal in a mouth that had never known manufactured horror.

But the unicorn would win the Chamberlain his master's grace. With the unicorn in hand, Rhu could ask for any boon and Landry would doubtless grant it – even immunity for Elsie, even the transfer of Elsie's person to the Chamberlain's keeping.

Rhu saw himself holding the woman he'd waited for so long, her amber hair rippling over his sleeve, her arms encircling his neck, her head resting in the hollow of his shoulder.

And what would buy this happiness? Only what he was giving, anyway. Only the life of a rare and mystic creature, betrayed to agony and death by the deceit of an apparent innocent.

chapter 2
SANCTUARY

"What's keeping the fool?"

Elsie beren Devona rested against the trunk of a live oak, just inside Fiddlewood. Brady would be back with supplies – soon, she hoped – and the end of her flight could begin. It was real only now, now that her only link with home was out of sight, now that she approached the border of her country.

How much longer to Kozabir? She hoped Brady's estimate of three or four days was over the mark. She was itchy with sweat and dirt and her feet never stopped hurting. She wanted a hot bath, scented with rosewater and sweet herbs. She longed for clean hair. She was weary of this rough male costume she wore to disguise herself. She ached for clean clothes – women's clothes – and soft, thin-soled slippers on rush-covered floors.

Elsie's sharp little chin trembled. Her lips, pressed firmly against a sob, turned down at the corners. Tears as large and soft as summer rain-drops patted onto the dry, crumbled leaves.

Far-off shouts and the frenzied barking of a dog alerted Elsie to present troubles. She sat up and dried her face with her dusty sleeve.

A blond young man in brown homespun came hot-footing into view from the south, two burly farmers in close pursuit.

"Brady, what have you done?"

Elsie made a quick search for a cudgel. She could at least deal with the dog; then she and her guide could divide the men and lose them in the wood. Brady may have brought this on himself, but she felt she owed him a rescue.

Brady turned to parallel the forest and led the men past where she crouched, where he must have known she waited. He took to the woods, the men not far behind. The dog belled after them and one of the men came back out and called it in.

Elsie heard a roar, then screams and yelps, and Brady's pursuers popped into the open like so many corks released underwater.

The younger man cried, "Bear! Bear!", as if a Citizen's Volunteer Bear Brigade were trained to answer that alarm.

Elsie dropped her club to cover her mouth with both hands, stifling her burst of laughter. She sank back onto the ground, weak with the end of her courage.

What could have gone wrong? Had Brady defied her and tried to steal when they were so close to away? Had he made some slip or stepped into a pile of plain bad luck? Well, she would ask him; no doubt it would be quite a tale as he would tell it.

Meantime, he had led the men away from her, and would be heading back to the river through the woods. She only hoped he had actually acquired some food for his pains.

Elsie stood, looped her nearly-empty pack over her shoulder, and jogged along the road, which soon dwindled to a cart-track and then to a footpath. Her chest burned and her side cramped. Her speed dwindled along with the road.

The light grew less and less. It became difficult to see the path, then impossible. Even the river showed only as a pattern of moonglints beyond the brush and trunks of trees.

Still there was no Brady, and no sign of him. Elsie stopped, and where she stopped, she sat. Where was he? Surely no farther ahead than this. He must still be behind, waiting for her. She should go back....

But not tonight.

Stupid, to make such makeshift plans. What way was that to see someone to safety?

With a groan, Elsie stretched herself across the path, closing her eyes against the little that was visible. If Brady came along in the dark, he would stumble on her. If something else came in the dark... let it come. At the moment, Elsie didn't care.

She fell into sleep, a deep and dreamless blank.

Above her, a tree's leaves moved, and whispered, "Ssshhe...."

Elsie sat up, her ears straining to hear beyond that whisper, knowing that she was listening, but not for what.

Something was on the path, and it wasn't Brady. It was something ponderous, with a tread that was weirdly light. Elsie couldn't hear its feet against the ground – she felt its tread. The weight of it – the *energy* of it – thrummed up the path like a hammer striking a harp string.

Elsie scrambled to her feet, clutching her pack as if she could defend herself with it, feeling the fool as she did it. She slipped off the trail, away from the river, where the trees and the darkness were thicker.

The thing moved in the same direction and came nearer. The trees and stones that blocked and baffled the girl seemed no obstacles to whatever approached her.

Its presence came before it. – No, not its presence. The presence of something Other, filtered through it. The Other surrounded Elsie; the air was thick with it. It held no Good. It held no Evil. It simply and dreadfully *was*.

The thing approaching held that Other within itself; it was all that kept that Other contained. It also kept that Other focused when It's nature was diffused, like a dam with a weir that turned water into power.

Elsie could feel the heart of the thing approaching. Its beat counterpointed the beat of Elsie's own. Its lungs drew her breath and let its breath be drawn into hers – the feeling was heady... delirious.

And the name she gave her response to this was "terror." "Terror" rejected the thing; its heart and its breath and the Other it barely incorporated. "Terror" freed Elsie to find her way back to the root-knotted path, to feel her way along it, away from whatever was coming.

Softer than a breeze, she heard, just at the level of hearing, "You have nothing to fear."

It wanted no more than that to trigger Elsie's panic. She threw herself straight ahead, caroming off trees, stumbling and tripping in a headlong flight that lasted no longer than a minute. Then she whirled into emptiness and over the bank into the Fiddlewood River.

~*~

She woke to the quiet hum of bees, to sunlight on one eyelid and damp sand beneath her bruised body. Something with a dull point pressed into her back. It shook her.

Elsie opened her eyes.

"Alive, boy?" said a voice as gritty as the beach.

Elsie gathered her limbs under her and rose slowly to her knees, brushing the muddy sand from her face with the back of her hand, shaking loose the pack still twisted around her arm.

The "beach," she now saw, consisted of a narrow strip between the water's edge and a grassy overhang of a few inches' height. The River washed up behind her as she faced the grass; it flowed past on the right and the left, with the forest beyond it on either side.

"Fell into the River, did you?" said the gritty voice. Elsie looked up.

On the grassy overhang stood a most peculiar-looking old woman. A loose black gown, blousing over at the waist, covered all of her but her milk-white hands, face, and neck. Even her hair was tucked up into a black and white turban, twisted into a squashy knot in the front. Her eyes were the color of blue light seen through green gauze, so bright they snapped like flaming raisins. She leaned on a blackthorn stick, having succeeded in poking Elsie awake with it.

"I didn't fall," said Elsie, "I was driven."

"By what?"

By what, indeed. Some creature of the Kinninger's? Of his mother's? Some creature of the wood?

"I don't know."

"What was it like...boy? What did it look like?"

"I don't know. I didn't see it, I felt it. It was... terrible."

The old woman grinned, her lips only a blush of color, her blocky teeth ivory against the pallor of her skin. "Was it?"

"...Yes." Strong, uncontrollable, larger-than-Life – that meant Terrible, didn't it?

"I'm Moder Zglaria," the old woman said.

"I'm...," Elsie began, and stopped.

The old woman said nothing, but gazed at the mucky figure with those translucent eyes as if content to wait indefinitely.

"My name is Edelin."

"Edelin beren Moder, I have no doubt."

"...Why do you say so?"

"Edelin beren Who, then?"

"Edelin beren...." What would be her matronym? Not her own.... Not her mother's.... She used the oldest and most distant she could think of: "Edelin beren Cinnie," she said, her claim made weak by hesitation.

"That'll do." The old woman extended a hand of opaque white, with only a thought of pink on the palm and beneath the nails. The thick white fingers closed over Elsie's slender ones. Elsie was surprised at how warm the chalky skin was, and how satiny, like the petals of a white rose in summer sun.

"You're on Wild Ass Island," said Moder Zglaria. "From the look of you, you were dragged here through high grass and rough country."

"I was." She stood and let a wave of dizziness roll over her and away.

"Hungry?"

"Yes. I want a wash and something to eat. I can pay. In silver, if you like."

"I'm agreeable to silver."

Elsie reached into her bag. She shook it off her shoulder, knelt with it, and turned it out. Only one purse. A purse of coppers.

She ground her teeth in rage, remembering how easily Brady had given way to her when she had refused him money.

"Robbed," she said. No wonder she'd found no sign of him. No wonder he'd led the chase away from her: Away from her was where he wanted to be.

"Fetch me some water and gather the goats for milking and I'll grant you food and shelter. I'll find you a clean gown to wear, as well."

"A gown?"

"Just until your manhood can be cleaned and dried, 'Edelin beren Cinnie.'"

Elsie considered throwing herself back into the River. If this old hag betrayed her, as Brady had done....

"Go or stay," said Moder Zglaria. "Please yourself." She turned and walked away.

After a moment, Elsie rose and followed her. What other course was there? – Starvation? Drowning? Exposure to what walked the wood by night?

The old woman gave Elsie hot water and a pot of liquid soap. She gave her a gown, of good material but torn and travel-stained. She gave her a cheese and an apple and a mug of goat's milk and a series of curt commands. Moder Zglaria asked no questions and offered no comments. She might have been blind to Elsie's gender, except that she was clearly blind to nothing.

When her traveling clothes were clean and fire-dried Elsie put them on. The old woman wrapped the gown in a length of homespun cloth and tucked it into a chest carved with long-tailed birds.

"Sit on the floor by my feet," she said. "Your hair needs doing. Only girls wear their hair loose in these parts."

So Elsie sat and the old woman combed and braided, turning the amber cloud of Elsie's hair smooth and tight and the color of earth. Four plaits hung over each shoulder, their ends fastened with scarlet beads.

When Elsie drew Moder's water and looked into the brimming bucket, she hardly recognized herself. The new lines of her hair changed the shape of her face, and the bright red beads shaded her eyes to cinnamon. Was this chance, or was the old woman helping to hide her?

It hardly mattered to Elsie, so long as she was safe.

Safe, but in basest servitude. The old woman laughed at copper and demanded payment for her hospitality in usefulness. The lowly abilities Devona had taught, in spite of Darcy's protests, bought Elsie's life and safety.

Sweep, scrub, hoe, milk, churn, glean, cook, tidy.... She would have left the island – she thought of it often – but she also thought of beginning life in a new country with only a small purse of coppers to sustain her. She would have to take employment as base as this, or worse, and in a foreign land, and with the fear of Landry's hearing of her somehow. The silver would have bought her safety, or passage to a land beyond her bridegroom's influence – but the silver was gone. So she did as she was told, grudgingly, grumbling, as poorly as she dared.

Moder smoked and showed her blocky teeth, not seeming to mind when the bread was half-baked or the corners dusty.

After some days of this, Moder sent Elsie below for a bottle of home-made wine.

"Fetch it from the right-hand shelves," she said.

The right-hand shelves were four steps distant. The left-hand shelves were within arm's reach. So Elsie took the left-hand wine.

Moder poured a glass and handed it to Elsie. "You could use a tonic."
Elsie drank, and nearly retched. "Vinegar!"

"Oh, surely not. I keep the wine that's gone to vinegar on the left." The old woman corked the bottle and left it on the table. "If there were as much value in spoiled people as there is in spoiled wine, the world would go on much better than it does."

Elsie's work improved – a bit.

Then, one night, she woke and couldn't return to sleep. Moder was restless, too, her hands and voice giving tokens of unquiet dreams.

Elsie rose and dressed and left the cottage. The moon was new and showed as the faintest sliver. Her heart spoke to her in the dim light, in a voice devoid of hope, in time to a slow and painful beat, like the thud of muffled funeral drums. *You cannot run from so powerful a man*, it said. You mean nothing, but the insult of your running from him cannot be ignored.

A glow the color of a lightning bug's appeared and grew. The glow came from the well. Not from the rim, but from the depths.

Elsie went to the well, her knees weak but her resistance weaker. She leaned over and looked in. Beneath her own reflection she beheld the face of a monster.

The face was large and bluish-green with a long, rounded muzzle and sharp white teeth. The eyes were huge puddles of darkness. As Elsie stared, the eyes narrowed. Bubbles came from the mouth, rose to the surface of the water, and broke into steam.

Elsie threw herself backward. She ran to the cottage, but stopped outside the door and looked back.

Vapor curled and drifted above the well in the glow from the monster's face. The glow faded and winked out.

Had it been searching for her? Having found her, had it gone to report? Had the report of the thing she had met in the woods set it on her trail? The night's disquiet, Moder's troubled dreams, monsters of land and water – surely, all were part of a threat she drew after herself as a bird might draw a poorly limed net, trapping everything that settled near it.

Elsie turned on her fear and seized it by the throat. She would not run to Moder Zglaria for help no one could offer. The old woman had done what she could do, and doing so had summoned danger to her island. She deserved better than entanglement with someone else's doom. Elsie owed her that much, and she would pay that debt.

She rested her palm on the cottage door in farewell. Then she slipped across the yard, through the trees to the edge of the grass.

The tide was out; the beach was wider than she had first seen it, the far bank was nearer. Moder had said the river could be waded at such a time, and Elsie waded it and climbed ashore.

She hadn't gone far before she knew she was being followed. On the bank behind her, something moved among the trees. She couldn't see it, but she recognized the feeling and the focus. It was the something that had driven her into the river.

She stopped and faced its coming. "I've left the island." Her voice rang clear in the still air. "Let the old woman alone."

The stars grew brighter, pierced the darkness, and traced a silhouette.

The thing among the trees was animal – monstrously large, of impossible bulk – unthinkable, that it could move so silently. The lines of its oddly-balanced body were forceful and broad. Only such a column as its neck could support such a head, wide and long, of odd proportions in the imperfect light. From the center of its forehead, from between the heavy brows, from a base as broad as Elsie's hand, thrust a spiral horn.

Unicorn. But when had "unicorn" meant such a beast as this? A plowhorse would seem a colt beside it. Its hooves were the size of dinner plates. It was the color of lead in the dimness. The whole world was the color of lead. Its eyes reflected silver, and the light seemed stronger in the reflection than in its original beams. It was terrible, indeed. And it was beautiful.

The creature's own presence overwhelmed the Other that it carried. It enveloped the girl. Not masculine, not feminine, not both, not neither, it enfolded her; it included her. It was strength defenseless. It was tender ferocity.

This was no slave of Landry Oliva, nor of his sorceress mother. Arrogance would sink in this presence. Authority would melt. Commands would wash away like marks on wave-lapped sand.

Again she felt the rest between her heartbeats filled with the beat of the creature's heart. She felt its breath in her lungs, richer than normal air.

This time the name she gave to her response was "love."

Again she heard it speak without a voice, and it said, *Help me.*

"I?" whispered Elsie. "How?"

Go back.

"To my home? To *him*?"

To Wild Ass Island.

"How will that help you?"

The beast was silent.

She wished she hadn't questioned it, but felt no anger from it, just a stillness between the question and its answer: *They'll find me through you.*

"Who will?"

Hunters.

Elsie had read the stories, seen the illustrations, of how to catch a unicorn. She thought of the simpering maid, caressing the prostrate head, while a man in hiding grinned and raised his sword....

"You must go away from me! Or let me go away! We'll separate, and let them follow me away!"

You must go back to Wild Ass Island. Quickly. Please.

"Yes. I will. I'm going. But.... It's safe for Moder Zglaria, if I go back? Should it be safe for her, and is it?"

Don't be afraid for her.

"I'm...." Elsie trembled in the all-but-darkness. "I'm afraid for me, too."

I give you my protection. It touched its horn-tip to the crown of her head.

The outline of the unicorn dissolved in starlight. The woods and the night were empty. Elsie shivered.

She waded back – the water was above her boots by now – and squelched across the cottage yard. The well stood dark and silent.

Inside the cottage, she spread her clothes before the fire. She put another log on and pokered up the flames. By the fire's greater light she saw that Moder Zglaria was still, her breathing even.

The next day, Elsie threw herself into her work. The corners were not just clear of dust, they shone. She sneezed and coughed, thanks to the night's wetting. Her eyes and the tip of her nose were red and swollen. Still she worked, until she moved with the awkwardness of strained muscles and Moder Zglaria ordered her to rest.

"I'll draw the water first," said Elsie. She felt a moment's qualm, but dismissed it. The memory of the "monster" in the well was gone.

Gone, too, was the memory of who she was. She woke as a nameless girl living on Moder's charity, dressed and named as a boy for Moder's reasons. She had always lived on Wild Ass Island and the old woman gave her no reason to question her state.

That afternoon Moder was restless again. She walked around the yard, toward the edge of the clearing closest to the causeway, back to where Elsie sat shelling dried peas as she rested, then back to the edge of the clearing.

Suddenly, the yard was alive with goats and geese, bleating and trumpeting someone's arrival.

Moder sat beside Elsie and lit a pipe. "Stay close, boy. Go in when I go in and stay until I leave."

"All right." Elsie's voice came in a croak. Her red-rimmed eyes were rheumy. Her nose was clogged; her mouth hung slightly open, giving her the look of a simpleton. "My head is buzzing."

"I'll speak twice, if I need to," said Moder, in a stronger tone.

A man came through the screen of cedars. He was tall, broad-shouldered, narrow at the hips, with chestnut skin and blue-black hair braided for hunting. He was dressed in a huntsman's short green tunic, close-fitting trousers, and soft-soled boots. He had no weapons. A waterskin, a food wallet, and a plain leather halter with a new steel bit dangled from his belt.

He bowed a courtier's bow.

Moder let out a puff of smoke as the animals' noise subsided. "Welcome to Wild Ass Island."

"I thank you." The man crossed the yard and sat on his haunches in front of her bench. "May I fill my bottle and buy some food from you?"

"Get him some water, boy."

Elsie took the man's waterskin, filled it at the well, and returned it.

"Poor game, then?" said Moder. "What kind of huntsman is it who can't feed himself?"

"I'm not hunting for food." Almost inaudibly, he said, "May the hunting stay poor for what I'm after."

"Be careful," said Moder. "Wishing may make it so."

The man's eyes met Moder Zglaria's and were captured by them.

"I'm Rhu beren Robia," he said, "from Kudasad. And you're called Moder Zglaria. I heard of you in Pazni. I've just come from there."

"They couldn't sell you food in Pazni? Why should you come to me with an empty wallet?"

"I made the mistake of telling them my mission. ...I'm hunting the unicorn."

Elsie continued shelling peas, as if "unicorn" and "warthog" were all the same.

"When I told them that," said Rhu, "they suddenly had no food or even water to spare me. They told me to come tell you my mission."

"And you came? Didn't you think they might be sending you into danger, Rhu beren Robia?"

"Of course I did."

"And yet you came."

Rhu shrugged. "Danger is everywhere."

"That's a wise answer. Come in and sit. The boy and I were about to have our tea." She raised her voice. "Let's have our tea, boy. The gentleman will join us."

Elsie looked at Rhu with the cold appraisal of an ostler calculating how much feed a horse will take. "All right," she croaked.

Rhu rose and helped Moder to her feet. Inside the cottage, he sat across the table from her, letting her smoke in silence, idly watching the "boy" limp and fumble through "his" tasks.

Abruptly, Rhu said, "I'm looking for something else. Some*one*, that is." When Moder remained silent, he continued, "A woman. Just fourteen. Delicate, dainty, graceful…. Her hair is the color of topaz, and it never stays in its fastenings. It's always…," his hands twiddled in the air beside his face, "…floating. Her eyes are round and brown, like her mother's – but you don't know her mother."

"How do you know who I know?"

"Devona beren Valda? Do you know her?"

"Only by reputation. I know her husband: Darcy Aminta beren Valda. He's The Crown Roll-Keeper."

"Why, yes. How amazing!"

Moder grunted. "You're easily amazed."

"Elsie – the woman I'm looking for – is missing. She's nowhere to be found. – Thank you," he said to the "boy," who had just served him a plate of buttered bread smeared on the rim by "his" grubby, snag-nailed hands.

"Did her mother send you, then? Or her father?"

"I'm looking on my own. For her. My Lady Oliva beren Audre sent me for the unicorn."

"What would she do with a unicorn?"

Rhu didn't answer directly, but he seemed to have no more appetite.

"And what would you do with the woman?"

Rhu didn't answer that directly, either. "She was to wed His Grace. I love her. Perhaps I wish I knew where she is so I'd know where not to look."

Moder leaned across the wooden table. "Don't look in Fiddlewood for anything. You don't know what you'll find. There's my advice. Take it or not, as you please."

Rhu stared into his plate. There was no sound but the crackle of the fire and the wheezing of breath in and out of the congested lungs of the "boy".

"I can't start back till the moon is on the wax."

Moder leaned back, grinning around her pipestem. "You can stay here. Fetch your horse from Pazni. We'll bed you down in the breeding shed; it's out of use at the moment. The boy will see to it. A piece of gold or so won't come amiss. I had a disappointment in silver recently."

The man stayed for a week. He spent his days wandering in the wood, coming back at dusk hungry and exhausted, eating enough to keep himself alive and sleeping deeply. He hardly spoke.

Elsie continued to suffer the effects of her night in and out of Fiddlewood. She hardly seemed aware the man was with them. He and his huge black horse might have been the same for all the difference she made in them; they took different fodder, that was all.

When the moon reached its first quarter, Rhu gave Moder Zglaria two gold pieces and rode away.

As the old woman stood outside the cottage, listening to Rhu's horse clop across the causeway, Elsie stepped into the yard and drew her first clear breath in seven days. "I think I'm over it." She stretched herself with animal suppleness. "...I feel as if I missed our boarder altogether. Who was he?"

"He was no hunter," Moder said, and chuckled. "If he didn't know his own true love when she served him bread, what makes him think he'd know a unicorn when he saw one?"

CHAPTER 3
BIRD OF THE MOON

When Farukh had returned to Granitz in Kozabir five times and the slave girl Nerissa birn Matka was nearly eleven, her mistress, Isa birn Isa, became ill.

"Medicine costs money, and so do doctors," Barand told his wife, in a tone that grudged the expense.

"I'll get better on my own," said Isa.

"You'll get better faster with help. I see it as an investment."

"Investment! We're kept poor from your investments!" Isa's voice rose, thin with weakness but hot with resentment. "Every penny I make –"

"And every penny I make, too," Barand pointed out.

And every penny you know I make, thought Nerissa.

Isa fell into a familiar litany of complaint: "If we saved it, or even spent it –"

"I spend it on the future."

"What future? Where is the future you've spent it on? Every thief and scoundrel in Kozabir knows you for their fool."

Ill or not, Isa birn Isa fell into bed, the print of her husband's hand across her face.

"We'll have to sell the girl," he said.

As usual, they spoke of her as if she weren't there.

Nerissa kept her eyes lowered for fear they would see how dearly she would love to be sold away from "home."

"Not the black market," Barand said. "Too much trouble. I'd have to bicker and dicker with them or they'd rob me blind.... No, it would take too long. We need the money now."

Isa sat up, rubbing her cheek. "Where, then?"

"It'll have to be a pleasure house."

Isa laughed. Then, sharply, she said, "Does she interest you, my husband?"

"Not as she is." He didn't seem to hear the sharpness.

Nerissa was the size of an eight-year-old but she had the face of one who had seen more than her years should have shown her. Her big-boned frame seemed all sticks and knobs beneath skin the color of cold porridge. Her eyes of dark blue looked larger for the shadows under them. Her red-brown hair was usually dull with grease and dirt; it was clean at the moment, and short, the birn Isas having just cut and sold its length.

"But they'll take care of that," Barand continued. "They'll wash her and fatten her up. She has some growing to do, yet. In the meantime, they'll probably let her wait on the older ones and learn from them."

Nerissa didn't look directly at the woman, but she saw her from the corners of her eyes. Isa birn Isa's face held an expression the girl had never seen on it before: a recognition of the girl's humanity and a trace of sympathy.

"She's just getting old enough to be some company for me," Isa said, half-heartedly.

"Let somebody else pay for that pleasure for a change," said Barand, and Isa turned away.

Barand took Nerissa out with him that night. He began with the richest establishment.

The house procurator looked Nerissa up and down, front and back, examined her hands and feet, and studied her teeth.

"Sorry," she said at last. "We're full up at the moment."

"She's a hard worker, Mistress," Barand said, over-oiling his rusty manners. "If you don't have a place for her up front, she could be useful belowstairs."

"Sorry," the procurator said, again. "It's not in the budget."

"Well, why didn't you say so in the first place?" Barand growled. "Took your time about it, didn't you? Do you think I don't have anything to do but sit around and watch you browse?"

The procurator had the two evicted.

If there ever had been a chance of Barand's doing the business he had in hand, his growing ill-humor would have ended it. He was turned away from house after house, often without being granted permission to show his "wares."

With every rejection, his grip on Nerissa's arm grew tighter and his steps grew quicker and more vicious, as if he could vent his anger on the stones beneath his feet.

"Please, Master, you're hurting me."

"I'll do worse than hurt you if you turn out to be worthless after all. What have I fed you for and sheltered you for all these years? Slaves are supposed to do more than earn their keep. Slaves are supposed to be an investment. They're supposed to turn a profit for you. Stand up straight and try to look like something human."

Human or not, Nerissa took no one's fancy that evening.

Before they had tried all the many houses of pleasure, Barand lost both temper and patience. "I won't go back with nothing. They say there are doctors who'll pay for fresh bodies...."

Nerissa had no fear of this old taunt and she was too tired to respond with the proper display of terror.

"You don't believe me?" Barand shook her.

"Master, let's go home."

"Do you give orders now?" He slapped the girl, thrust her into a lightless alley, and threw her to the ground. Doubling both his hands into fists, he waited for her to get up.

A voice inside Nerissa spoke as if it had been gathering itself for years: *Not this time.*

"Get up," said Barand.

Instead, Nerissa groped, clutched the first thing she touched, and pitched it at the man.

The thing turned out to be a cobble and it hit him with a solid *thunk.*

He staggered back, shook his head, and sat down.

Nerissa scrambled up and ran into the alley's blackness.

He was after her in a moment but his heavy boots were easy to hear and he had to stop now and then to strain for the sound of her bare feet.

She tried to choose her route but found herself taking the first turns and narrowest ways. She was away now, and the fear of being caught and hurt again outweighed her craft and caution.

Halfway down a passage between two warehouses, she knew she had lost her race. She knew where she was and she knew there was no way out. She ran to the wall at the end of the passage; she cast herself against it as if she would force her body through it. The brick was solid. No windows, no doors, its top at twice her height.

She huddled in the dark. Maybe Barand would miss this turn. If he only glanced in, he'd never see her.

She heard him stop. She heard the hiss of his boots on the gritty street as he turned. She heard him coming nearer.

To her horror, the passage lightened as the clouds thinned. In a handful of seconds, the moon would show her clearly.

Something passed her with a whir. From near the mouth of the passage came a trill of music more lovely than anything the girl had ever heard. A bird sat on a ledge of one of the warehouses, stretching its throat in song. There were no colors in that light, but the bird was pale, with long and drooping tail-feathers. Barand stared at it, too.

If only she could creep away while Barand was looking at it. Impossible.

But, in the moonlight, Nerissa saw the impossible could happen. There was a vertical crevice in the wall where none had been before.

Nerissa took to it like a rabbit to a warren. She had to step up into it and wriggle back.... And she was trapped. The crack went deep – deeper than most walls were thick – but it didn't open on the other side.

She heard Barand shout as he saw her go to ground. She saw him, through the cleft, pound toward her.

The entrance exploded with song and feather, as the bird returned. Nerissa could see, in a light the bird seemed to contain rather than reflect, that its beak and feet were yellow and that its feathers shimmered like liquid fire. Red, blue, black, glinting with diamond sparks. Its eyes...its eyes were blue....

Barand's grimy hand took the pretty creature by the throat. He snapped its neck with a movement of his thumb and tossed the corpse behind him.

Nerissa gasped, breathless with shock and fury. She braced herself and made claws of her hands, determined she'd leave her mark on that man if she paid for it with her life.

Barand put a foot up into the entrance of the crevice. Surprise and uncertainty brushed his face as he saw her braced to meet him.

Before either of them moved, there was a rush of brightness. Barand drew back, a spot of blood on one cheek. Another bird like the first perched at the edge of Nerissa's sanctuary.

"Killed your mate, did I? Well, don't be lonely." As he reached for the bird, it flew at him, pecking and clawing. His hands met around it and it fell dead on the empty stones. He came back to the pocket in the brick, to find another bird there trilling a silver war song.

"Don't let him –" Nerissa said. The bird was in Barand's hands before she finished, "– hurt you."

Barand's eyes met hers as he twisted the shining head.

Nerissa heard the bird's neck crackle as Barand broke it. She heard the little body hit the cobblestones but couldn't see past the new bird, the living bird, now blocking the way.

Barand cursed and knocked it aside. It fluttered up, stooped, and struck his ear with taloned feet. It drove its beak at his eyes. The man screamed and tore the creature off. His blood flew, black in the silver light. He slung the bird at the nearer warehouse.

Nerissa heard it hit but didn't hear it fall.

She worked her way forward until she could see all of the passage. There was Barand, mopping his ear and face with his sleeve, cursing in a whining drone. There were the stones of the street around him. She could see no shining feathers, no broken bodies. Yet he had killed four birds....

Barand stopped cursing. He had seen her standing unprotected. He lunged.

Feathers blinded him, steel hooks tore at him, the point of a living dagger dug into his face.

Shrieking, he grasped the bird, flung it to the stones, and crushed it beneath his foot. Still shrieking, he threw his arms up to cover his head from another attack.

When the singing started, Barand shut his mouth and lowered his arms. A shimmering bird sat in the entrance to the crack in the wall, its five long tail-feathers curled about its feet, its wings folded, music pouring from its opened beak. It was the only bird in the passage, alive or dead.

Barand stumbled backwards, swiping at the blood on his swelling face as if it contaminated him. At the mouth of the passage, he turned and ran.

The bird flitted after him.

Nerissa didn't remember wriggling out of the crevice. One moment she was in it; the next, she stood by the wall, which was once again unbroken.

I must have run my head into it – knocked myself out – dreamed the rest. She felt her head for tenderness or lumps but found none.

At any rate, she was free.

Dizzy with the thought, she crept from the alley and through deserted streets. Cautiously, she made her way to her cache and took it up. Only a handful of coppers, but better than nothing.

Now, where to? Farukh had just left town again; if she knew which way he had gone, she could follow him. As Barand had truly said, she was a hard worker. Maybe Farukh would let her work her passage to another life. She had no more to lose by asking, nothing but capture to gain by waiting.

Which way, which way? The joy of her release evaporated. Nerissa crouched in the abandoned garden, all the terror of eleven years upon her.

She was free, but she was alone and friendless. What if Barand had already recovered from his fear and was looking for her?

But she had forgotten – that had been a dream. Nothing had frightened Barand. He had simply passed her as she lay unconscious. He would still be hunting for her; and what if she blundered into him? What if he had enlisted his cronies' help in searching and they were all over Granitz? How could she avoid them?

A faint trill of song came from her left. It was the song of the bird, the heroic bird of her dream. Nerissa turned toward the sound.

The bird perched on a stone no more than a foot away. Its feathers glinted like light on water and blue sparks winked from its eyes. Its beak was parted as if in laughter, and the whisper of song slipped out for her alone.

"You're real…."

The bird flew once around her and lit on the garden gate.

Nerissa went to it.

It flew out and down the alley, waiting for her at the crossing of two ways.

Nerissa followed the bird through the moonlit city, not noticing or caring where she went. Crowds and single figures passed before her and behind her and through streets on either side, but any street she walked, she walked alone.

Buildings came farther apart. The surface beneath her feet turned from cobble into hard-packed dirt. The moon went down and Nerissa walked in darkness, nothing guiding her but the gleam of feathers flickering in the gloom.

Behind her, the sky turned faintly gray. As the world brightened, the bird grew dimmer until, with daybreak, it was not there at all.

She followed the road all day. All day she saw no other travelers, no houses, no hearth-smoke. She rested many times but could never sleep for fear of Barand or a Slave-hunter. She never cried and she never doubted her way; this was the road her bird had showed her. She would walk it to its end.

chapter 4
the baffled hunter

Leaving Wild Ass Island behind was like riding out of a warm fog into a cold, dreary day. Rhu's chief impression of his week's "hunting" was of fierce blue-green eyes in a linen face, like illuminations on bleached parchment. His long walks in the forest, the welcome-back of Moder's impudent stock, the old woman's short-witted serving boy – these were shadow memories, like fragments of a dream.

He had failed his lord. Guthrie beren Melanell would make the most of that failure. He might even be given the quest, himself. If so, he would succeed.

Rhu's mouth dried in fear at the prospect. He thought of Guthrie riding to Fiddlewood – red hair and rage – like a forest fire on horseback. Then he thought of Guthrie swaggering into Pazni, blatting his intentions and bullying the villagers. He thought of Guthrie coming face to face with the feral eyes of the old woman in the wood, and Guthrie's success no longer seemed so sure.

Rhu left the Fiddlewood near Pazni and rode through town, wanting it plain that he had failed. The unicorn, if it existed, and the legend of the unicorn, if it did not exist, meant a great deal to the people of Pazni. They had been cold to the huntsman but not brutal to the man; Rhu felt he owed them reassurance.

There were nods of satisfaction as he passed and, oddly, a few bows and curtsies. Rhu's stallion, Ebenos, swung his head from side to side at these attentions as if accepting them for his master.

Rhu turned his horse to the south and rode along Fiddlewood River's eastern bank. He slept in the open. The moon's increase was strangely comforting; its glow on his closed eyelids seemed to bring peaceful sleep.

When he came in sight of Kudasad bridge, the Chamberlain reined to a standstill. The stream of folk on foot, horse, or vehicle parted to flow around him, indifferent to him as he was to them.

Rhu was uneasy lately about his master's quality. Not that Landry's birth or breeding were open to question. The House of Sarpa was one of the country's oldest and purest of blood. The family records showed a line of descent so long one wouldn't have been surprised to see the first entries made on rock with burnt wood. There had been a Thane of Sarpa in that manor since Thaneholds had first been granted.

Still.... Part of Rhu beren Robia's work was to spot and weed out servants who didn't measure up. And how is one to deal with a servant who eases power from the grasp of an absent overseer and uses it to usurp that overseer's place? Rationalize it how one would, accuse Karol of serving the people ill by leaving herself open to that usurpation, was Landry's action that of an honest steward?

Must he go back? Must he return to service in a family whose loyalty seemed, increasingly, less to Layounna than to itself? Must he support with his efforts a royal line enthroned by questionable right and held by questionable practice? Why not turn away, and leave his House, his country, his ambitions and his scruples in the dust at his horse's heels? Lose himself in Fiddlewood, or Kozabir, or some land beyond the borders of Layounna's neighbors?

He could not. He was still Landry's man and a man of Landry's House. Service to Sarpa was still, to some degree, service to Layounna, and so the answer was no. Or perhaps the answer was no because Hayward Oliva beren Ada (a decent boy – a wholesome man) was also of Landry's House, and was married to a living beren Ada, and held himself apart from the rest of Oliva's poisonous brood. Perhaps it was because there was a hope that Elsie was still in Kudasad and might resurface and need him. Perhaps there was only this urge, pulling at him, drawing him across the bridge, and all the other perhapses were merely rationalizations.

Once across the bridge, Ebenos developed a limp in his left front leg. Rhu dismounted beside the road and gently pressed a hand to the horse's pastern. Ebenos lifted his foot obediently but then, on three legs, limped out of Rhu's reach.

Rhu rose and followed. Ebenos left the Fiddlewood River Road, struggled around a low hill, through a crescent of willow and fruit trees, and into a clearing. There, he stopped. Rhu inspected the favored leg from hoof to withers; nothing was wrong with it.

Ebenos lowered his "lame" hoof to the ground and began to graze.

The clearing was lush with grasses and wildflowers. A snug-looking little cottage of wattle-and-daub nestled in the herbage between the trees and the river.

Not far from where Rhu stood, the Fiddlewood River Road pulsed with traffic; here, all was peace. The only sounds were birdsong, the gurgle of the river, and the suspiration of the wind. The sun was high, and the warmth of it went to Rhu's bones and spirit.

A raucous cluck cut across the quiet as a fat black-and-white hen flurried from beneath one of the trees. She flapped her wings in an unconvincing challenge and ran to shelter.

"News! News!" Rhu heard a voice from beyond the hut say. "What is it this time, Chandler? Did a bird land on a branch? Did an apple fall off the tree? Was there a breeze? Eh?"

Rhu went toward the voice as the voice neared him. He came in sight of the cottage door as a tightly-muscled, white-haired man reached it from the direction of the river.

The man's dark face was framed by crudely trimmed hair, an even more crudely trimmed beard, and a drooping moustache. He was dressed like a churl, in ungartered ankle-length breeches. His blocky chest was bare, as were his feet.

"Excuse me," said Rhu. "My horse went lame. He seems to be better now. May I rest him here until I'm sure he can go on? Under the trees?"

The old man's full lips spread in a shining smile. "You have permission and welcome, My Lord Chamberlain. You made my ease your business, once. Now your ease can be my business and I'm glad of the chance."

"I… know that voice, but…."

"Can you imagine me bald?" the peasant said. "Can you imagine me harnessed to the lightest cart in the bailey, in a tunic with 'Liar' painted on the back?"

Rhu's jaw dropped. "By all that's wonderful! Andrin beren Tooli! So this is where you ended."

"Not yet. I haven't ended yet."

"Nor will, for a good long time, I hope!" Rhu clasped the old man's hand. "What has it been? – Ten years?"

"Thereabouts. It seems like yesterday but, yes, it's been about ten years."

"We thought – *I* thought…. It was if the earth had swallowed you up. I looked for you, later, but I couldn't find you, nor any word of you. I was afraid…."

The old Waymaster opened the door and led Rhu inside. The hut was lit with a warm orange glow, flickering from a stone fireplace and from a dozen or more rush candles. Yet, though the one room was windowless, the cozy air was fresh and filled with briskness.

The hen came with them, settling herself in a corner, in a nest lined with strands of the old man's silver hair.

"You were afraid," Andrin said, "that Landry had done in secret what he was afraid to do openly? Had me killed?"

Rhu frowned. "My Lord would do no such thing."

"Of course not. We weren't speaking of what he might have done, though, but of what you thought he might."

"I couldn't tell you what I thought, precisely. …I was uneasy." The Chamberlain's face was softened by one of his increasingly rare smiles, as he said, "You'll never guess who counseled me not to worry for you."

"Young Biddi beren Anna. Though I suppose 'young' is relative. She told you I was away and safe and that I'd come back when I was called."

"How did – I've been told I'm easily amazed, but how did you know? Did your Vision tell you?"

"Biddi told me. She's always been able to find me. She comes to see me, now and then – keeps me current. Still a kitchen maid, she tells me, and I tell her she's lucky to be that. She credits you with keeping her free and working."

"True, in a way. I wish I could claim kindness or generosity but it's policy, really. The villeins are not content with Landry's regency. Biddi says what they all think and feel but dare not say, and says it from a low enough position for Landry to ignore her. Biddi's the crack in the lid that keeps the pot from boiling over. I see protecting Biddi from herself as part of my job."

"That's what Biddi claims. There are different opinions about that, though."

Rhu was about to ask what Andrin meant, when the old Waymaster turned his head and said, "Yes, if that's all right."

"I beg your pardon?" said Rhu.

"I'd be honored if you'd share my midday meal, Rhu beren Robia."

"That would please me very much."

"Hot food or cold?"

"Whatever you provide. I could get dinner anywhere; only here can I have your company."

After a pause, Andrin said, "Yes, very well put." He took the inverted lid off a three-legged kettle which sat on the hearthstones apart from the flames.

"Isn't that your old temple pot?"

"Yes, and more serviceable now than when I used it to mask the scents of the world around me." Andrin pulled out two small cheeses encased in yellow wax, a bowl of boiled and salted eggs, a round loaf of dark bread sliced nearly through and stuffed with butter, and a bottle of golden wine. "Dandelion," he said, waving it gently. "To celebrate."

Rhu took the things as Andrin handed them to him, and put them on the table. Andrin took plates and glasses from the mantelpiece. There were two of each, Rhu noticed. "One for you and one for Biddi?"

"Sometimes. I have other company."

"Do you? Who?"

"I have relatives, you know. I didn't spring from a void. I have a family like other people." After a pause, he said, "Well, perhaps not *quite* like other people." Andrin glanced away again and said, "You've been keeping odd company. Besides myself, I mean."

"How did you – Never mind. Yes, I have. I've been in the Fiddlewood. On a quest to capture a unicorn, if you can credit me with such romantic business."

"Oh, easily. Only a romantic man could serve a household so unworthy of him. – No, don't glower at me. I suppose I may speak as freely as a kitchen maid. And what I say is, only a house of utter foulness would send a man like you as bait for what they aren't fit to take themselves. Only a line as corrupt as tainted meat would even think to ruin innocence with innocence. Isn't that the quest they set you?"

"Allow me to relieve your mind about it. I failed. Thanks to my ineffectiveness, no harm was done. Or perhaps I'm not as innocent as others seem to think."

The angry flare left Andrin's black-purple eyes and the dusky knots of his fists unclenched. He chuckled. "My dear young man, that's all that saves you." He turned his head again. "I'm right, I think?" he said, and nodded.

"Who is that?"

"Who is what?"

"You're talking to someone. Who is it?"

"You mean you can see her?"

"No." He didn't think Andrin could see "her" either, but it was clear the old man thought he spoke to someone.

"Can you hear her?" said Andrin.

"No, I cannot."

Andrin seemed to listen for a moment. "She doesn't want me to tell you who she is. She says you aren't ready for that yet. She says that when you're ready, she'll show herself to you."

"Who will?"

"She will."

After a moment, Rhu nodded. Andrin smiled, and they ate heartily, in companionable silence.

When they had finished, Andrin said, "She wants me to tell you a story."

Rhu pushed aside his empty plate. He leaned his elbow on the table and his cheek on his hand, with a sigh. "Tell me her story, then."

"Once," said Andrin, "there was a man who lived near the river. He thought the river should flow, so he got a piece of wood and he carved a paddle. He stood on the bank and pushed at the water for hours. When he grew tired and his arms weakened, he dropped the paddle into the water. The paddle was carried away. A triumph!"

Rhu waited for Andrin to continue, but the Waymaster only sat beaming at him.

"Thank you," said Rhu, at last. "I must be going, now."

Andrin nodded. "Go in the peace of the Way. I'd rather you didn't tell anybody but Biddi that you've seen me, but you must please yourself about that."

"If Biddi can keep a secret, so can I. She'll speak of this before I will."

~*~

Rhu rode on, glad to have something besides his failure to think of, though the something else was somewhat less than cheering. His relief at finding the former Waymaster alive and healthy was bound up with sadness at the old man's mental decline.

He remembered Andrin as he had been on his last day in the bailey. He saw him standing alone before that row of hostile faces in the Great Hall, his cheeks flushed and his finger trembling as he prophesied doom and doom and doom. He saw him at the bottom of the storeroom steps, calling himself a liar, sagging beneath the weight of his banishment. He saw him framed by the storeroom doorway, staring at the well as if something marvelous had come out of it and had popped back in before the Chamberlain entered. He saw him outside his temple, fearless and venomless, defending the man who was packing him off from the vengeance of a kitchen maid. He saw him, finally, laughing at the Chief Sword's spite, which few would feel moved to do and none other would dare.

"A better man than your master," Andrin had said. Rhu had denied it, and had meant the denial honestly. But how deeply had he meant it? In the framework of Society, he was beneath his master, but so was the old man. Was Landry Oliva a better man than the man he'd failed to shame, the man his bullies had failed to terrorize? If not, was he a better man than his Chamberlain?

And now, what had Landry's punishment done to the old man? This invisible and inaudible person to whom Andrin spoke, that so-called story he had told, his habit of storing all manner of food jumbled together in one pot.... Andrin was fortunate to have a friend like Biddi to check on him now and then, and to keep him supplied with hens – at the castle's expense, no doubt, but there'd be no trouble made about that. "Chandler".... A daft name for a chicken. One more sign of the poor old fellow's woolliness.

With Biddi so much on his mind, it didn't surprise Rhu to find her standing just outside the city's boundary wall, yet he felt he was seeing her for the first time in years.

She was heavier than he remembered her being. Her auburn hair was now closer to the color of toasted wheaten bread, the red tones grown pale, the dark strands shot with yellow-white.

She lifted a hand in greeting. "I had one of my feelings you'd be back today. I seemed to see you with the sun on your face, and everything behind you in your shade."

"I'm not the man for that. I cast a small shadow." He came very near to telling her he'd seen Andrin, but remembered his vow and kept the secret even from her.

"No unicorn." Biddi pinched her rosebud lips between her teeth, trying to hide a smile.

"I hope My Lady Oliva finds half the pleasure you do in my failure."

"You didn't bring her back a unicorn. That's not what I call a failure."

"My Lady will sing me another tune. And it won't increase in sweetness with waiting. May I take you up behind me, back to the castle? Or are you on your way to somewhere?"

"I was waiting for you. But we'd better go back separately, for your sake. Still, I thank you." Biddi put a large, rough hand on the pommel of Rhu's saddle. "Let me go first. Give me time to get to the keep before you come. I... I'd like to be there, when you tell her."

Rhu frowned. "Is it My Lady's anger you want to see, or is it my disgrace?"

"Oh, no, neither. I thought... I thought you might like to see a friendly face, afterwards." She lifted her chin and said, defiantly, "Now, laugh."

Rhu laid his hand on Biddi's, making hers seem small. "Go first, then. I never laugh at kindness. It isn't common enough to be amusing."

The Chamberlain took his horse, at a slow walk, along Broad Street, parallel to the city wall. When he came in sight of the Roll-Keeper's manor house, he stopped.

Devona beren Valda's shop sign hung nearly motionless. The door stood open, but Rhu couldn't see inside from his position.

Did Devona know where Elsie was hidden?

Landry and the others clearly considered Devona little better than a fool – a fit companion to the dullard, Darcy.

Rhu disagreed with them. That lively face, those owlish eyes, flashing behind those thick round lenses, that head always turned or cocked toward anything that warranted attention – those were not the features of a fool. If Elsie had disappeared through friendly machinations rather than those of the Kinninger, Devona knew about it or was capable of making a very shrewd guess.

Rhu walked his horse slowly past the shop.

Devona looked up from her copydesk as the Chamberlain passed. Their gazes met and held until reflected light hid the scrivener's eyes from view.

By Oliva's standing orders, Rhu beren Robia was brought to the Great Hall in all his weariness and dirt. He found Oliva pacing, her time-lightened skin dark again with fury. She whirled to confront him, shaking her small fists.

"Is this how you serve me?"

"Yes, My Lady. Always to the best of my ability."

"You have failed me, Rhu beren Robia. You're a poor huntsman, to come back empty-handed."

"I went, and walked in the Fiddlewood, just as My Lady suggested."

"And found it empty?"

"Empty of Unicorn, My Lady. I stayed in the 'Wood itself, at the hut of an old woman. She had a sickly, cloth-headed man-servant, geese, bees, and goats. In all of Fiddlewood, I met only these and caught glimpses of only everyday forest creatures. No one and nothing else."

Oliva stepped close to the Chamberlain and stared up at him, as if she would see through his skull and into his memory. "There came a time when you were hidden from my Vision. There is some power at work…. If you should prove to be in league with it…."

"In league against my own House?"

"In league against MY House – the House you serve."

Rhu's face, schooled by his life, did not alter in expression.

Oliva glided to her seat, at the left side of the throne.

"I am… disappointed." Oliva gave the mild word a hiss and a spit that it usually lacked.

Rhu felt a chill – familiar from his childhood – run down his spine. Years of efficiency and self-effacement stood between Rhu, the man of position, and Rhu, the boy who had borne his lady's disciplines; those years melted in a heartbeat. Rhu felt again the icy bath of cruel words thrown at him in public, remembered the time he had been leashed and muzzled and led on his hands and knees one muddy afternoon while his weeping mother watched.

"My son will also be disappointed," said Oliva.

Rhu resorted to something he hadn't done for years: he offered an excuse, not quite keeping the plea from his voice. "It was never certain a unicorn still exists. One can't bring back what isn't there to be brought."

"That may be. That *may* be. But *something* exists. Something stands between my Sight and the things I wish to see…. Whose mist obscured you from me? Am I to believe you met no one on your quest but a feeble old woman and a thick-witted churl? Or am I to believe the power that opposes me comes from such rubbish – and all the way from Fiddlewood, at that?"

Rhu thought again of Devona beren Valda, and wondered again what and how much she knew.

Oliva sat forward and extended her hands. "How am I to defend myself, if I am friendless?" she said, her eyes blinking as if they were weak with age or tears.

Rhu knelt, took her hands, and kissed them, loathing the gratitude that moved him, shocked and appalled by the loathing.

"I depended on you in this," Oliva said. "I had no one else to trust with this mission. If your faithfulness has failed, who have I left?"

"My Lady...." Rhu's tongue tumbled over itself in its eagerness to form words the Thane would like to hear. What could he tell her? What had he to offer her? "I heard tales of unicorns. Everyone told me stories, but all the tales were fantasies, heard from the same storyteller. Farukh, his name is; I've heard him many times."

"And did you meet this storyteller on your mission?"

"The people say he's left the country. He had been before me more and more recently as I traveled north. In Pazni, they told me he had planned on crossing the Inland Sea for Kozabir."

Oliva shook her head. "It would take more than a scuttering mountebank to obstruct Tarkastrian arts. You stopped at no Waystation on your journey?"

"No."

"You met no Waymaster? Or Waymistress?"

Andrin. He had met Andrin. That would appease her, and turn her displeasure elsewhere. She might not send Swords for the old man, but be content with devising rituals to counter his imagined interference. Or she might send Swords and they might have no more luck in finding Andrin than Rhu had had when he had deliberately looked.

If that weren't good enough, he could tell her about Biddi. Biddi could lead the Swords to Andrin, or pay for her defiance if she refused. The woman was a traitor to her House – or, as Thane Oliva would have it, to the House she served.

And what was he, hesitating even this fraction of a second over his reply? Didn't he owe his Mistress the knowledge she sought? Didn't he owe her an honest answer?

Rhu raised his head.

"No, My Lady," he said. "I met no such persons. Knowing My Lady's distaste for the Way and its followers, I purposely avoided Wayfarers. Was I wrong in this?"

"No."

Before she could speak again, Rhu said, "Mightn't it be your own powers that concealed me? It could be the only important thing about my going was the proof that there is no living unicorn, if there ever was."

Oliva beren Audre sat back, her fingers slipping from Rhu's cold clasp. "No living unicorn," she said, with regret so real and soft only her intimates could guess what a living beast would have endured at those little hands. "Then, if I cannot have the use of its parts and powers, neither can anyone else."

Rhu remained on his knees while his Mistress forgot his presence. When she noticed him, idly, her unfocused gaze touching him by chance, she dismissed him with a gesture.

The Chamberlain rose on weak legs and left the Great Hall with what he hoped was less wobble than he felt.

He stopped on the landing, and saw Biddi on her way down the stairs to the storeroom.

"I need that friendly face," he said.

The face Biddi turned to him was so masked with pity and contempt, Rhu flinched. "You knelt to her," said the maid. "She couldn't have put me on my knees before her with a club. And I'd have bitten her fingers off before I'd have kissed them."

"You weren't taken from your parents and raised to do it." His father, who had disliked sending his youngest to be a whipping boy, was long in his grave. His mother still served Sarpa at Oakwood. He paid duty visits to her, now and then. "You'd find it easier to play humble, if you had been trained as I was."

"That wasn't an act."

Rhu had no answer, except that an act would not have been convincing, and even he had trouble understanding what he meant by that.

So Biddi turned her back on him and descended, and he mounted the stairs to his chamber.

He had changed.

At what point had it happened? When had he stopped truly thinking of himself as Landry's man and secretly become his own? When had Oliva and her House become a "them" and not a "we", and when had Landry's enemies turned "friendly" for the Chamberlain? For nothing less had happened, despite his protests to himself and Andrin and his endless My Ladys to Oliva.

He picked up his shaving razor. He pulled his hunting braid taut. One moment… two…. The braid hung from his hand, his silky blue-black hair as coarsely cropped as Andrin's silver mane.

The Chamberlain looked into his heart and knew that, if nothing else stood between Thane Oliva and success, there stood Rhu beren Robia.

chapter 5
SALALI'S ÓARGAIN

"You're late enough getting back," said Kinnan, as Trahern hung his soft hat on a clothes peg. "Brady and I already ate – We were about to go back to the forge…." The sentence trailed away in the face of Trahern's apparent disinterest.

"Excitement in town," said the smith. He sliced and buttered a round of bread.

Brady birn Ilka dipped up a bowl of beef and barley and handed it to him. "Aren't you going to tell us what it is?"

"Yes. But I'm going to have my dinner, first."

Trahern showed the others the blank of his hairless head. He ate as if his teeth were hammer and anvil and his food were as tasty as glowing iron.

Trahern was in his fifties, now. His skin, the color of straw packed into a bale, was still smooth, the hair on his arms and in his sparse eyebrows still entirely black.

Kinnan and Brady sat across from each other, at the left and right of Trahern at the head of the table, and wondered.

Excitement in town, Kinnan thought. *Excitement that's turned Trahern in on himself. Swords*? Kinnan's fists clenched and he felt the sudden thrill of rushing blood. With effort, he steadied himself. It couldn't be Swords. Trahern would never sit here, calmly eating his dinner, if Swords were in Vatra.

When he could stand the silence no longer, Kinnan asked, "What is it, then? Trouble?"

"Most likely."

"For me?"

"Most likely."

"For you?"

Trahern raised his head and looked Kinnan over: the short, dark-blond curls, the gray eyes, the sprawling nose. "Not for me. I've served my purpose, and gladly. Now that's most likely done, and there it is."

"Do I know what you're talking about?" Brady asked.

"It's that storyteller," said Trahern. "Farukh."

Kinnan felt as if the air had been sucked from the room. "In Vatra?" Time. It was time.

Trahern nodded.

Kinnan rose from the table, his hands not knowing what to do with themselves.

"Careful," Brady said. "You nearly put your fist into your bowl." Still rawboned and gangly at twenty-odd years, Brady took comfort in others' occasional gracelessness. "Not very heroic."

Kinnan looked at Brady as if he hardly saw him. Then his eyes warmed, and he sat again. "Did you speak to him?" said Kinnan. "What did you say? What did he say? You didn't.... It might be better if no one knew about...."

"I know how to keep my wits about me. I listened to one of his stories...something about a unicorn in a pit, and a lion –"

"Never mind the story. Go on."

"When it was over, I waited for everyone else to clear away, and went up to him. 'I know a story you might use,' I said. 'It's about a young man waiting for a friend who's a long time coming.' 'That's a sad story,' he said, 'if that's the ending. Suppose the friend comes, after all, with news the young man wants to hear?' 'And takes him away, into danger?' I said. 'Well,' I said, 'That's his business. My business is blacksmithing, as you can see. My forge is just outside of town – ' and I gave him directions for getting here. 'Maybe you'll stop in before you leave,' I said, 'and tell that story to a young friend of mine.' 'Maybe I will,' he said. 'Or maybe I'll send someone else with a story he'd rather hear. A true story.'"

"Salali?" Kinnan asked. "Was there a woman there? An older woman – well, younger than you, but older than me. A Nishite?"

Trahern shrugged. "I didn't notice."

This was the second time Kinnan had asked after Salali. Neither of his companions questioned his interest any more than they questioned his interest in the bruised child in Granitz. It was something to do with his quest for Layounna's throne, they each supposed, which made it no business of theirs.

"Today…." said Kinnan. He stood again. "We'd better pack."

"We?" said Brady.

Kinnan hadn't spoken of his intention to retake Layounna for his mother's line since the night Brady had first come. Brady had refused to help him then, but Kinnan had somehow assumed that he had changed his mind. Now Kinnan stared at him in disbelief.

Brady shook his head. "No."

Kinnan made a disgusted sound and began stuffing his few belongings into his old pack.

"I told you," Brady said. "I told you I wouldn't do… whatever it is you have in mind for me to do."

"I don't have anything in –"

"And how can I go back to Kudasad and tell my Mistress I lost her daughter in Fiddlewood and left her there?"

"You didn't, man. How could you help –"

"And what if word gets around that I'm a friend of Kinnan beren Ada?"

Kinnan's long-banked anger at Landry fused with his new disappointment. "Consider yourself safe, then – that word would never go around. And if it did, I'd give it the lie. You're no friend of mine – coward."

"Coward?" Brady stood, black eyes snapping, feet braced. His slight figure grew larger; his muscles swelled and hardened. His fingers, ordinarily slender and dexterous, thickened as they curled into fists.

Trahern smacked the table so hard the wooden dishes jumped and tumbled. "None of that. Vary your shape for violence and I'll fling the poker at you."

Brady returned to his proper form, but his look of sullen rage remained.

"It hardly matters," Kinnan said. "A varier might have been useful, but one that's all show and stealth and no heart… that would be worse than nothing."

"That's the royalty in you," Brady said, "that calls a man a coward because he won't risk his neck for you. You could've asked Elsie if I'm a coward, if you had bothered to really look for her while I couldn't do it myself."

"I looked for her."

"You didn't find her."

"And you would have, I suppose?"

"I'd have died before I'd have given up. Coward, yourself!"

"Stop this!" said Trahern.

"*I?*" said Kinnan. "I can't afford the luxury of dying in a lost cause...."

"Oh, can't you?" said Brady.

"Another word from either of you," Trahern rumbled, standing and gripping the table with hands like vises, "and I'll throw you both out the door. By the Mother of Life, I will."

Kinnan and Brady gave him long looks, as if each were weighing the risk. Then Kinnan returned to his packing and Brady cleared the table.

There was no easy conversation at the forge that afternoon. Kinnan alternated stretches of furious work with long minutes in the yard, trying to outstare the horizon. Brady tidied the cottage and came to the forge to fetch and carry for the smiths. When idle, he pulled tunes from his pipes to the rhythms of their hammers. No unnecessary word passed anyone's lips.

Brady's thoughts were occupied, as they often were, with certain dreams and visions. More than once, since that time on the road with Elsie, Brady had seen a reflection or caught a glimpse of a roan-haired young woman with dark blue eyes, only to turn and find an empty place where she had been. More than once, since that first night lost in Fiddlewood, he'd dreamed of her. He saw the colors of her embroidered palla in the flames, in the flowers at the forest edge, in the sun on the underside of clouds.

Who was she? She didn't seem to want anything of him. She didn't seem to be aware of him. It was as if someone were showing him an enchanted portrait, depicting the subject with the flush and movement of life. But who was the someone and what was his... her... its purpose?

Kinnan was haunted by harder thoughts. His time of waiting might now be over. Once again, he would have to leave the forge, the sweet smell of hot metal, the hard-won satisfaction of turning something unyielding into a shape to suit his will.

The light grew dimmer, the forge fire was banked, and the tools were put away. The three men went into the cottage.

A knock at the door startled Kinnan out of a dark reverie. He sprang up, opened the door, and there stood Farukh. His yellow hair and pointed beard and mustache shone in the cottage light. His clothing – black and white and blue and red and yellow – seemed riotous, after years of plain Vatran homespun.

His companion made him look dull. Salali barely reached his shoulder. She was dark and small and swathed in brightness, draped in gauze and bangles like a dried date wrapped in gift paper.

"You must be Salali," said Brady. The woman flushed and smiled, her teeth white in her dark skin, her expression young on her aging face.

"Greetings and blessings on you all," Farukh said, bowing with a flourish. "Many thanks for your gracious invitation, friend smith –"

"You have news for me?" Kinnan interrupted.

"Take them to the forge and get your news," Trahern said flatly. "Brady and I have no part of it."

Kinnan started out at once, his eyes cold and his lips set.

Salali opened her mouth as he approached, but he signaled her to silence.

"We can speak more freely outside," he said softly. "These people have been friendly enough, but they're not entirely sympathetic to my aims."

Salali let Kinnan past, and went into the cottage. Farukh followed her, leaving Kinnan alone on the porch.

"I require witnesses," Salali said. "There was to be a bargain, remember?"

"What news do you bring?"

"There was to be a price."

"How can there be a price? How can I pay you with what I haven't got? – Is it a promise you want? Would you be satisfied with that? All right. If you help me gain the throne –"

"Overthrow Landry," the woman corrected.

"It comes to the same thing…."

"Say it as I say it."

"…If you help me overthrow Landry, you may name your price. Anything that's mine to give or in my power to do is yours, so long as it doesn't hurt my people or my honor."

"You heard him," Salali said to the men. "You're my witnesses."

"It's not a bargain I'd have made," Farukh said. "Still, I'm witness to it."

"Yes, all right," said Brady.

Trahern nodded.

"The news," said Kinnan, still on the porch.

Farukh stepped further away from the door. "Not so abrupt, Master. Come in and sit down. We've been a long weary way, and we want a soft seat and a mug of beer if there's any to be had." He rubbed his hands together like a man anticipating a great delight. "We've been offered hospitality in a strange land and that's not something to be brushed aside." He cast an indulgent look down at the woman. "Is it, my fellow wanderer?"

"Kindness should never be refused," she said. "In the taking or in the giving."

Brady offered the woman his seat with a flourish and pushed a stool nearer the fire for Farukh. He cocked an eyebrow at Trahern, who nodded, then he drew some of the weak local beer from a keg in the pantry and brought it to the guests.

Kinnan came in and kicked the door closed behind him. "When you're quite settled and comfortable…," he said, with heavy grace.

Farukh took a long pull at his beer, his blue eyes twinkling at Brady over the rim. "Patience is considered a virtue, Master," he said, over his shoulder, to Kinnan.

"He's being patient," said Brady. "He hasn't called you a name, yet."

"Rebellion's in the air," Salali said, as if nothing had passed since Kinnan's first demand for news. "You can smell it and taste it, like the aroma of someone else's dinner. Landry took another bride and keeps her locked in a tower—"

"That's a lie," Kinnan snapped. "Unless he's taken a third wife. That girl, Elsie: she got away from him."

"Do you know this?"

Brady bowed. "I got her away."

"Did you, indeed, Little Master?" Farukh combed his beard with his fingers, his smile flashing briefly. "That would be a tale worth hearing."

Brady sat on a footstool, clasping one fist in the other and scowling at his hands. "She got away from me, too. I lost her in the Geiskeflor – or Fiddlewood, as her people call it."

Salali grunted. "No one is lost in the Geiskeflor, whatever you call it. If she was there once, and she hasn't come out, she's there yet. You may never find her, but she's there."

"What do you mean?" Brady shook his head in disgust. "Oh, yes. You mean those old tales about spirits and whatnot snatching stray mortals. Naturally, you'd think of those if you've been traveling with Farukh."

"Not all tales are false," Salali said. "No more than they're all true. But the people *think* the girl's still in the castle, and they want to see her. They don't have the courage to demand it yet, but the anger's building."

"They're starting to speak of Landry as a tyrant and a usurper, using the tools I've given them to say it." Farukh put his mug on the floor and spread his hands, using his fingers as lightning rods to draw his listeners' attention to his face. "They start with my stories," he said, in his market-place voice, "then make up their own. By talking in riddles they know the answers to, they can talk openly – and they do." The storyteller sat back, eyes crinkling as he broke his own spell.

"You should hear them," Salali said. "I've only been traveling with Farukh this past week; before that, I followed him, swimming in his wake, if you will, and seeing what his passing stirred. The tales the people tell themselves lack Farukh's elegance –" Farukh bowed, "– but they have their own power." She gestured to Kinnan. "You're 'the rebel, Kinnan-called-beren-Ada', and you're as cruel as you are slippery."

"That isn't –" Kinnan began, but Salali spoke over his protest.

"You always perform your outrages on Thanes and government officials. Occasionally, they tell how Kinnan-called-beren-Ada spared the life of somebody's father, or rescued an old woman from persecution, or delivered a love-letter for someone who didn't recognize him."

Kinnan made a face, and Brady laughed.

Salali smiled wanly. "Those are my favorites, those love-letter stories. They always happened to somebody the teller knows well, of course–"

"A monster and a clown!" Kinnan broke in. "That isn't how I want to be thought of! I'm the heir of Onagros, not –"

"Idiot!" said Brady. "'Bane of the powerful, servant of the weak' – What more could you want? I told you, the country is more than half in love with you; cruelty, kindness, and all. Worry about how nice you look after you're safe in power. What did you think you would do? – Come back already crowned?"

Salali drank her beer in silence while Kinnan adjusted what he wanted to suit what he'd been given.

"I never found that girl," Salali said, at last.

"What girl?" said Brady and Kinnan, together.

"The little girl," Salali said to Kinnan. "The one who warned us of Landry's sneak attack."

Farukh's bright eyes rested gently on the woman. "You thought to look for her?"

Salali said, "I've been working my way down through Layounna and back to Granitz. The whole circuit takes me about eighteen months. Just finished my fourth. Every time, I look for the girl, but I've never seen her again. I thought I did, once, in the marketplace. She had the right color hair."

"Roan," said Brady, but so softly no one heard him.

"I could see bruises on her face and arms and legs, but she didn't even look at me." She cast a glance at Kinnan, but he wasn't looking at her, either.

"They've killed her, then, the brutes," said Kinnan. "Killed her body or her spirit – and I know which is worse."

"We'll never know who 'they' are," Salali said. "But the Mother of Life knows."

"'The Mother of Life.'" Kinnan curled his lip around the words.

"Is that how you Royals do it?" said Brady, with heat that tried to look like ice. "Sneer at beliefs you don't happen to share? Elsie was only the daughter of a stationer and a jumped-up records clerk, and she had more–"

"Enough!" said Trahern. "The man can't help his blood, Brady birn Ilka. Twit him again on it, and you leave."

"He can help his manners, can't he? He isn't very noble, if you ask me."

Kinnan stared at Brady long and hard. Then he smiled joylessly and bowed. "I'm sorry. You're right. I apologize to all of you, and to the Mother of Life. I wasn't raised to be Royal, but I was raised to be civil. I'm sorry I was rude. – And don't think I don't know what burr you have beneath your saddle, Brady birn Ilka. I take back 'coward'. I take back asking you to put yourself in danger for another country's Kinninger. I have no right, and you have no responsibility."

"No, I don't. Not to you."

Farukh's bright blue gaze rested on the varier. "What do you plan to do, then? Stay here for the rest of your life? Lose yourself in Kozabir?" When Brady didn't answer, he said, more softly, "Lose yourself in Fiddlewood?"

Brady frowned until he was certain he wasn't being mocked, and said, "I plan to go back and search some more."

"But why, lad?" said Trahern. "I thought you agreed it was too late. What good can come of it?"

"Maybe I can find what's.... Maybe I can find what's left of her. I owe her that, at least. And then I'll know. Maybe I'll write a letter to her mother. Maybe I'll be able to make myself go back and tell her face-to-face, once I can tell her something certain."

"But–"

"He's right," said Kinnan.

Brady and Trahern both looked at him in surprise.

"I see you need to do it," said Kinnan. "And there was some truth to what you said, about my search being…. Well, it was a thorough search, as far as I went. But…. I can go back to Layounna by many routes. If you'll have me, I'll go with you, down through Fiddlewood. Your Elsie wasn't on the west bank of the river, and she wasn't above the river's curve. We'll ford the river at the Northern Shallows and look along the east bank, going south. Maybe she crossed, somehow…."

"And then what?" said Trahern.

"Then he meets me in Pazni," said Salali. "I'll go down that side of the Inland Sea, through Bahari. Landry's made trade agreements with Kozabir that hurt the people there. I'll see if they're ripe for revolution yet."

"They're ripe." Farukh sat forward, drawing the others' interest. Kinnan felt a familiar pre-battle cold at the base of his spine. He could all but smell the leather, horses, fear. "The partisans Landry has put in charge of the districts are underlings, not administrators. They wield their power with more enthusiasm than discretion and have lost any popular support Landry might have commanded." Farukh turned his hands palms-up, and they saw Landry's strength trickle out between the fingers. "People are gathering arms. They claim it's for defense: Istok mercenaries have been raiding across that long eastern border and Landry seems to wink at it." The storyteller glanced up at Kinnan, and smoothed his beard. The mood of the room lightened. "Just harassment and a touch of looting, so far; no blood or damage, but plenty of costly and undignified mischief…."

"If I could get those mercenaries to harass the Swords and Thanes instead of the farmers and shopkeepers, and do it in my name…. If their tales of me came true, I wonder how that would sit with the people."

Salali chuckled. "It would sit well. And I have safe passage back and forth across the border, and access to the mercenary camps. I'll meet you in Pazni, then, and let you know what the Captains have to say."

"I can't promise them safety."

"If they wanted safety," said Farukh, returning to his beer, "they'd be silversmiths."

~*~

Farukh said his farewells and moved on, but Salali accepted Trahern's offer of a bed for the night. The weather was mild, and she requested a pallet on the porch. She dreamed again of the mirror, Kinnan within it, staring past her; Farukh behind him, beckoning her forward. She woke confused, feeling abandoned and bereft, as though her heart's desire had departed and it was only a friend who slept nearby, instead of the other way around.

~*~

When Kinnan and Trahern went to the forge the next morning to put the finishing touches on a two-man job they had in hand, Brady followed them as far as the porch and lingered there.

The trinket-woman sat cross-legged, a wallet of materials unrolled on her lap, fashioning dreams out of wire and beads.

Finally, Brady said, "Salali...."

"Yes, lad?"

He eyed her pack with hungry curiosity. "I've heard of you, you know. They say you make charms to suit any need. I need...." He shook his head and started over. "What would you do if you were in love with a dream?"

Salali breathed a deep sigh and motioned for the young man to sit beside her.

He continued: "I dream about this woman. I see her – just barely... and I don't know her."

"Maybe she's a wish, lad."

"Maybe she is," said Brady, unhappy at that possibility.

Salali opened her pack. She sorted through her goods, and pulled out a bit of silver, pinched between blunt thumb and forefinger.

"Here, take this," she said, kindly. "Wear it."

Brady held out a hand. Salali dropped the bauble into it. It was a loop of heavy silvery thread, tied in a love-knot, with a hook at one end. Brady eased the hook through one of the holes in his ear.

"What will it do?" he asked.

"Let's just say you'll find your sweetheart."

Brady ducked his head in thanks too deep for words.

"I can't pay you," he said. "I have silver coin, but it isn't mine – it's Elsie's or my Mistress'. These are mine, though." He fished in a pocket and pulled out a pair of silver studs. "I bought them with my first wages in

Kudasad. Take them."

"I don't ask –"

"Please."

Salali nodded and took the studs.

Kinnan and Trahern came back.

"Aren't you ready yet? I only need my sword."

"I'm ready," Brady said.

"And I'll be on my way," said Salali. "But first, let me repay your hospitality."

Trahern pushed at the air, rejecting the idea. "I'm no inn-keeper. You were welcome to everything you had here."

Salali held out one of the ear-baubs Brady had given her. "This doesn't look like much, but it's tremendous wealth: half of someone's worldly goods."

The smith looked from the bauble to Brady, one ear hung with a new loop and one ear bare.

"Such a treasure is too rich for me to keep to myself," Salali said. "Take this half, from one maker to another."

Slowly, Trahern extended his palm, and accepted what he was offered.

~*~

When their visitor was gone, the men gathered in the cottage for awkward goodbyes.

"If Salali owes you a gift for one night's lodging," Brady began, "I can't calculate what I owe."

Kinnan nodded. "Or I."

"None of that," said Trahern, his voice becoming gruff. "Young Master Kinnan, you've more than paid your way with me. And as for you, Brady, your music and antics have been better than a play. I think there's something owing on *my* side of the scale." He opened a cabinet made into the wall. "You don't know where you'll be or how long you'll be there, or what you'll have in your wallets or.... Well, here's some things for you. You'll take them."

"What sort of things?" said Kinnan, but the slowness and softness of his question betrayed his hope of what sort of things they were. "Special things?"

"Useful things," Trahern replied. He passed the items to Brady, who ranged them on the table. "A cooking pot full of hot food when you're hungry. A loggerhead that pokes wet wood to flame. A lantern that shows the way through darkness, fog, or thicket. And a sword."

Kinnan balanced the sword in his grip, holding its blade in his palm, turning it to admire the even play of light along its perfect edges.

"Be careful how you use it. Young Master, be very careful. Some swords cut more than flesh and bone."

Kinnan nodded. "The sword I came with is an old friend. Will you keep her for me?"

Without a word, Trahern went to the shelf where Kinnan kept his sword sheathed and wrapped in his traveling cloak. Still without a word, the smith unwrapped it. There was a trace of silvery powder on the cloak's lining, a sheath, a swordbelt, but no sword.

"It was there when I used it to get the balance and dimensions for the new one," said Trahern. "It wasn't there when I came to make sure the new blade fit the scabbard."

"Someone took it," Kinnan said, uncertainly.

"Who? I don't need a sword."

"Steel and I don't mix, you know," said Brady.

Kinnan's hand embraced the pommel of the sword the smith had made for him. "Well, then," was all he said.

"Remember my warning," said Trahern. "Choose your targets carefully. That'll be Life your sword will be taking. Life."

"I understand," said Kinnan, but he didn't.

~*~

Once more alone, Trahern went back to the forge. By the light of a lantern, he set himself up for silver-work. He opened a straw basket and lifted out an empty bird-cage. It was made of silver filigree, too clumsy to look like lace but still very graceful. It was small – no larger than a skep – a straw beehive – and utterly impractical. He had begun it when Kinnan first came, as an application of techniques the silversmith taught him, but it had taken on its own imperative. He dug Brady's stud out of his pocket and soldered it into the design, then closed down his small forge. He took the bird-cage in with him, falling asleep with his hearth-fire coloring the filigree rose and yellow.

He dreamed of a man, even larger than himself, with matted black hair and a hooked nose.

"After the Mother created the Divine Four," the man said, "she created one more person. Not divine, but a First Creature, nonetheless:

Man, the Maker. She made it, then divided it into male and female, and bound them to the earth. Once or twice in a generation, somewhere in the world, a human is born in harmony with the elements. That person becomes a Maker of extraordinary things – music, tapestry, painting… iron goods. A lot of the Makers have been smiths, probably because they work with all four elements: air to pump the bellows, earth to give the ore, fire to heat it, water to cool it. You're one."

Trahern felt dizzy, lost. "Why me? What is my purpose?"

The man laughed harshly. "There speaks a human for you! That's something no one can tell you. You were given a nature. You weren't given a purpose. If you want one, you have to find it for yourself."

In the morning, he woke to find a rainbow in the cage.

A bird sat on the perch that had been empty the night before. It was no larger than a hummingbird and its feathers had a hummingbird's iridescence, glinting with diamond sparks as the light touched just so. Its small, pointed beak and its feet were yellow. Its eyes were the blue of a summer sky. Its five tail feathers drooped in sweeps and curls of yellow, red, blue, white, and black.

"Does it sing?" asked the smith, with soft and tender voice. "Does it talk?" He poked a huge finger into the cage not far from the sharp little beak. "Does it bite?"

It seemed to do nothing but sit and fluff its feathers occasionally and yawn, showing a tiny pink tongue like a bit of ribbon.

Trahern took his butterbread and ale in silence. He offered the bird some bread, but it paid no more attention to this offering than it did to the smith.

The act of offering bread to the bird brought the idea of sacrifice to the smith's mind. Perhaps this still, silent creature had been sent to him to be given in sacrifice to one of the Divinities. Tortoise was the Divine Animal most revered in Kozabir – Perhaps Tortoise had sent the bird, and expected it to be returned to him. The bird promised no struggle. It would be easy to think of it as a willing victim.

Trahern, accustomed to judging beauty and balance of line, appraised his prisoner. It was a thing of perfect grace. Even without song or movement it produced an invisible but palpable glow – a living glow that passed from its heart to Trahern's.

While he spoke in soothing tones the bird continued to ignore, he picked up the cage and carried it onto the porch.

"Go on." He opened the cage. "If Tortoise wants you killed, he'll have to catch you. I hereby offer him – or any Divinity who's interested – the gift of your freedom, but not your life."

The bird poured out like milk from a pitcher; its long tail and the eye's memory of where it had been an instant ago turned it into a liquid streak. Its shifting colors paled in the sun's harsh light, and it was gone before Trahern saw it was going.

chapter 6
sorcha forsworn

Sorcha beren Ada – now called Sorcha beren Moder – knelt in the women's garden of Kudasad Waystation, pulling green onions. She loved the homely odor. It comforted her, even as she blinked back tears for the memories the pungent smell invoked....

Karol, the elder princess, had a natural bent for statecraft; as the younger heir, Sorcha was allowed to slight those lessons and indulge her taste for the domestic. She sat in on her share of Courts and Councils, but she much preferred the kitchen.

The younger princess was twelve when her mother died and Karol took the throne. She was fifteen when the sons of Thane Oliva beren Audre offered themselves in marriage to the royal sisters, and sixteen when she accepted for herself.

Hayward beren Oliva, the younger son, the one who laid siege to Sorcha, was a plump, formless-looking man, with pudgy hands, a soft mouth, and eyes of muddy brown. The delicate features of his mother, sister, and elder brother were overwhelmed by his heavy chin and pillowy flesh. The fine kink of his sister's hair was fuzz on his round head.

Sorcha wept, that he was the first whose suit her life had allowed her time to entertain. She raged, that Karol was courted by Landry – the handsome one, the dazzling one, the one with charm, address, and a merry nature.

Hayward talked of little but crops and cattle and the needs of villeins. When he took Sorcha on excursions, they rode to Sarpa, Oliva's Thanehold, or his grandmother's Thanehold of Oakwood and inspected wells and fences.

Sorcha was her mother's daughter, and this attention to the common welfare worked on her as insidiously as ivy on stone. It was with a lighthearted young woman's despair that Sorcha realized she loved the dull dog and wanted no-one else.

When Karol accepted Landry's suit and the new Kinninger's Consort took his mother and sister with him to the castle, Hayward became his mother's and grandmother's bailiff and he and Sorcha moved to Sarpa Thanehold.

Sorcha was the mother of four when the life she loved crumbled like withered leaves. When the forest retreat where Karol rested from her duties went up in flame, so did Sorcha's peace. Then worse happened.

She was pulling green onions in the kitchen garden at Sarpa when Hayward came out to her.

His clothes clung damply to him; perspiration beaded his scalp and face and hands. "Wash and pack. As quickly as you can."

Shading her eyes from the sun, she peered into his face. "But Cook is plucking a goose for dinner. I haven't forgotten we were engaged for tonight, have I?"

"It's Landry. He wants me to bring you and the children to the castle."

Sorcha dropped what she held and leapt up, her face alight. "Karol!" she said. "Karol's been found!"

Hayward shook his head. "Landry says a young charlatan who calls himself Kinnan beren Ada – claims to be brother to you and Karol – is threatening the throne. Landry says we would be safer in the keep. I think otherwise."

Sorcha brushed dirt from her hands. "So do I. If the boy were truly my kinsman, we'd have nothing to fear from him. If he were not, he wouldn't dare harm us, for fear of proving himself false."

"It isn't the boy I fear. It's...."

Sorcha felt chill, as if someone had removed a protective cloak. "Landry? Your own brother?"

"Sorcha, blood does more than bind family together. Sometimes, what it binds is better slipped. Landry wants you and the children."

Stubbornly, refusing to hear the meaning in Hayward's words, she said, "I don't understand."

"Even though he knows you renounce all claim to the throne, for yourself and for our children–"

"I do, and you agreed. Does he want it in writing? I would put it in writing."

"Proof means more than paper."

"But what can I do?" she wailed.

"What can *we* do, Love?"

They held one another tightly, regardless of mud and smell and dampness.

"Why didn't I ask Andrin?" Hayward muttered against Sorcha's hair. "He only said I should do what I must. I should have pressed him for a clearer answer."

"He's a Waymaster," Sorcha said, with a reassuring pat. "It isn't in them to…." Sorcha fell silent.

"What is it?"

"The Waystation," Sorcha whispered. "We'll enter the Waystation, the children and I."

"Would they take you, knowing the danger?"

"There would be no danger, if they'll take us. And they will. They never turn anyone away. Don't you see? When we enter the Waystation, we leave the House of Sarpa and the House of Onagros alike. None of us could claim the throne, because none of us would have the right."

"Would they take me, too?"

Sorcha held Hayward's soft round face between her mud-streaked hands. "Oh, my darling. How could you leave your people? Not your family – your people. You're father to more than Vevay, Atwell, Joia, and Blaine. The Sarpa villeins look to you for their protection. I want you to come with us, but could you do it?"

Hayward raised his eyes, his arms tightening around his wife's body. "Yes."

"No."

After a moment, Hayward said, "I want to."

"You had much better stay here. You'll be close to us, away from the court but not too far away to keep current of what happens there. Your letting us go will seem, to them, as if you hold us in light regard…. You and the children and I will be safer for that."

So it was arranged.

The Waystation of Kudasad was the largest in all Layounna. It claimed fifty acres of ground north-west of the royal city, bordering part of Thane Oliva beren Audre's vast estate. Its unwalled boundaries were marked by fruit trees and berry bushes.

The main building, or Stationhouse, was set in the center of the acreage. It was built in the form of a capital letter E. The Eastern and Western strokes were dormitories, men in the East and women in the West. The central stroke housed the common rooms: work rooms, the dining hall, the kitchen, the temple. There were no windows in the central stroke, turning the open spaces on either side into gender-segregated gardens. In the connecting stroke were the infirmaries, the school-rooms, a lobby for the reception of visitors, and the administrative offices.

Waymistress Brina beren Moder gave over three cells in the first floor rear of the women's dormitory to Sorcha and her children.

When Vevay beren Moder turned fourteen, a match was approved between her and a cow-herd from Sarpa. Vevay and her husband took the gravid cow that was his bride-price and crossed the Kudasad bridge. When Atwell beren Moder turned fourteen, he left to seek his fortune. Joia beren Moder came of age and she left with six companions to found another Waystation. That same year, Blaine beren Moder, at twelve, was granted an apprenticeship with the Sarpa steward, working under the supervision of the manor bailiff – Hayward, the father he could no longer officially claim.

In the meantime, Hayward rode often to the Stationhouse. He spent hours supposedly closeted with Brina beren Moder or her deputies, supposedly contending over the boundary the Station shared with Sarpa.

Oliva approved Hayward's harrying of the Mistress; but, then, Oliva didn't know that Hayward gave Mistress Brina only money and "good day," and spent the rest of his time at the Stationhouse with his children and his "cloistered" wife.

He made an official visit to Sorcha once a year, on the anniversary of her renunciation, in the company of Oliva's estranged mother, Audre beren Oda. He reported to his mother and siblings that they spent those visits impressing on Sorcha the wisdom of her choice. In reality Hayward, his wife, and his grandmother passed the time in warmth and reminiscence.

It was far from an ideal existence, but it was existence, and few of those Landry saw as challengers could boast as much.

Sorcha soon turned the three rooms into Home. The peculiar, underhanded life wore into normalcy. Landry and Oliva and Corvina let her be. She saw no one from the court. She saw only Hayward from Sarpa Thanehold and Audre beren Oda from Oakwood.

Intrigue and blood and scandal flowed, like a river parted by an island, around the Waystation. Layounna moved unquietly under a skin of pressed peace.

Vevay was aware of it, and took her husband and her cow away from the capital, where she died giving birth to her first child, who did not survive her long. Atwell was aware of it, and left. Joia founded her Station on grounds as far from the royal city as she could buy. Blaine huddled under his father's wing with a trust no man could warrant.

Sorcha closed eyes and ears and mind and heart; she heard and pondered as little as she could. The world outside the Station had no meaning for her, except as it touched her husband and her children. They floated, for her, like bubbles on the surface of a pond; bubbles that would never burst, so long as she was conscious of them – them, and nothing else.

~*~

Hayward and the children respected her denial of the world and Audre beren Oda kept her peace on the subject. Waymistress Brina did neither.

Waymistress Brina beren Moder's long black wig was always slightly askew on her shaven head, and her Waymistress's yellow robe was always spotted with stains of ink or gravy, but the copper eyes in her ageless face were as sharp as new cider.

"They've banished Waymaster Adept Andrin beren Tooli from the castle," she said one day, in the year Vevay was married. "Hitched him to a cart and drove him out – with whips, I've heard it said."

"Master Andrin...." Sorcha raised a whitened face from her embroidery frame. "With Landry's knowledge?"

"By Landry's order."

Sorcha's look wavered, and returned to her sewing. "Well," she said, "let it be so. I suppose he's come here. I shall enjoy talking with him again."

"He's disappeared. I wonder," said Mistress Brina, in a voice that held no wondering, "whatever could have happened to a man who displeased the Kinninger and his mother?"

Sorcha's hands stopped their work, trembling, but she didn't raise her head, and the Waymistress left in silence.

Then there was news of a moonlit bloodbath in Andrin's old temple. It had been committed by the Kinninger against Swords called traitors for their supposed murder of Kinninger Karol beren Ada.

"It seems he's been misjudged," said Sorcha. "My sister is avenged. Let that be an end to it."

"He claims the throne for his mother's line."

"I wish him better of it than my mother's line has had."

But, saying this, Sorcha knew she lied. She sneered at herself, a Stationhouse Wayfarer, who disclaimed her inherited place with one side of her heart and coveted it with the other.

Better not to think of it. Better not to know.

Still, as year followed year, Brina brought her tales of Landry's self-stewardship. Tarkastrianism flourished, with Oliva's cultivation.

The mysterious Kinnan-called-beren-Ada haunted all corners of the country, then dropped from rumor into folklore. Some said he was taken. Some said he was hanged. Some said he was killed by treachery in Kozabir. Some said he had escaped – that he could not be caught and held. But stories of him never ceased, and grew with the telling.

These stories, Sorcha never tired of hearing, though she tried never to show it.

Landry took a consort, the daughter of the Roll-Keeper. Brina reported the girl was kept a prisoner in the tower. No one had seen her since her bridal day. Some said that Oliva had charge of her and was misusing her in some Tarkastrian foulness.

The muscles of Layounna, her churls and villeins, gathered themselves beneath her, ready to crouch and spring.

Sorcha pretended to herself and others that she did not know or did not care; that it was nothing to her.

But, oh! the glory for the people, if they should pull the Lion of Sarpa from its stolen lair – deal it the death it merited! And, oh! the loss of common, priceless lives!

Still, it was nothing to her – she had made it nothing when she had dissolved her matrilineage.

Then the storyteller began to come. Farukh, the storyteller, with his outlandish looks and his voice that moved through his words like a song through music.

When he appeared at the Station, even the cloistered Wayfarers came to listen. A door from each secluded garden led to rows of benches along the meeting room walls enclosed by fine latticework.

Farukh could spin his tales for hours, moving his listeners to tears of laughter or of pity. But always, before the end, would be a tale of unicorns.

There was a unicorn (the gist of one story ran) who, frightened by a snake, escaped onto a mountain, where it lived in safety. Below, it saw the other animals grow wasted, as the serpent's venom poisoned plant and water. The unicorn knew that one touch of its horn to anything would bring it back to health. But, in its terror, it had struck its horn against a rock to break it off, and the horn was lost. The unicorn turned its eyes away, but the cries of the dying animals filled its ears. At length, it descended, and stood before the serpent. The serpent struck, the unicorn died, and the other creatures tore their poisoner to bits in rage. Where the unicorn fell, the soil was sweet. Year by year, the sweetness spread, and ran with the rain into the rivers. At last the time came when all was wholesome once again.

It would have taken a duller mind than Sorcha's not to see Layounna in that story, and herself in that unicorn. She could not help but be stirred, but there was nothing she could do. She had been in the Station too long. She had been forgotten. It was too late.

Now Sorcha's skin, the color of tawny oak, was grooved at the mouth and crinkled at the eyes. Her thick, full hair, a mixture of honey, caramel, and cinnamon, was threaded with silver. It hung in round curls to her waist in the back, braided on the sides, the braids wrapped in the faded rags of her old finery. Her nails were short, her hands were calloused and held only the power it took to pull green onions.

chapter 7
waymistress

Brina beren Moder sat at a desk made smooth and white and undulant by more than ten decades of use and scrubbing. Across the desk, shifting in a chair as hard as the Mistress's own, sat the Kinninger's sister, Corvina beren Oliva. Corvina was in her middle thirties, by Brina's judgment – too young for her look of hauteur to be impressive, too old for it to be amusing.

When Brina only sat with folded hands and serene expression, Corvina opened a heavily embroidered wallet. She took a bundle from it, which she placed on the Waymistress's desk. The bundle was as big as two of her own slim fists, wrapped in cotton wool and tied with ribbons of brocade. "This is for Sorcha."

Brina beren Moder put the bundle aside. "You said you had business to discuss," she said, pleasantly.

Corvina's cheekbones flushed with rose. "What about the gift?" Her voice edged toward shrill. "May I give it to her?"

"Of course you may. You know her anniversary date. You could come with your brother Hayward and your grandmother." The Waymistress slid the bundle across her desk.

Corvina put her hands in her lap. She sat as if at ease, but Brina could see the small, smooth hands clenched in the fabric of the wallet. "Can you give it to her for me today?"

"Is that what you would like?"

"I'd like to do it myself, but…. Yes."

"Now, what business do you have with this Waystation?"

Corvina's almond eyes narrowed in a way more reminiscent of her mother than either of them would have appreciated. Her fingers uncurled and stroked the wallet's gorgeous panels, as if the matter at hand eclipsed all that had gone before it.

"Alicorn," she said. "You have some, here. His Grace my brother has need of some. The crown is prepared to purchase, but should you be unwilling to sell...."

Brina finished the sentence, maintaining her air of casual pleasantry, "The crown is prepared to take it, is that it?"

"For the good of the realm." Corvina smiled with her teeth. "But I'm sure such measures won't be necessary." She hardly knew which she would prefer: Persuading this Way-crawler to sell, or forcing her to give.

Either way, releasing the alicorn to the House of Sarpa meant the end of the House of Onagros, and the end of the Way in Layounna. One could almost feel sorry for the old harridan.

"'For the good of the realm' is a strong appeal. How much?"

Corvina took a small sack from her wallet and put it on the Waymistress's desk. "There's enough there to be of use to you. We do not haggle."

Brina permitted herself an open smile. "I meant how much alicorn do you need? We don't have many pieces."

"We want all of them."

"Less than a handful," Brina cautioned.

"A few pieces. So you've said. I accept that. We have a bargain."

Brina beren Moder rose and went to an upright cabinet of uncarved, unvarnished wood. She took from it a box, also unfinished and undecorated.

"You keep it in that?" said Corvina, her voice strained with disbelief. "So rare a treasure, you keep in a... in a pillbox? Not even under lock?"

"Things aren't treasures."

Corvina stretched out a hand, and Mistress Brina gave her the box. Corvina's fingers trembled as she opened the container, making the contents rattle, which made her tremble more. She put the box on the table, afraid of spilling what it held.

Three chips lay in the box, each no bigger than her smallest fingernail. They were as white as the heart of new ivory, with the sheen of mother-of-pearl. She lifted a chip between thumb and forefinger. Held between herself and the fire in Brina's hearth, the piece seemed to warm and glow like the flesh of a hand cupped around a candle flame.

"So fresh.... I've never seen any so white. Where did you come by these?"

"They've been here longer than I have. Will those be enough for your purpose?"

"Enough. More than enough."

"They're yours, then. Or the crown's, rather. Keep the box. Was there anything else?"

"No." She closed the box with great reverence and tucked it into her bodice. "But you won't forget my present, will you?"

"I won't forget."

"And I won't forget, Brina beren Moder. You've served the House of Sarpa well, keeping our brother's wife these ten years. You've served us well again, in this. I promise you, it won't be forgotten." *A sword to the heart instead of something lengthy – there's a reward.*

When the Kinninger's sister had gone, Brina looked out of her office and motioned to a male Wayfarer in homespun trews and tunic. "Follow My Lady Corvina. Come back and tell me when she's off the grounds."

When this was done, the Waymistress regarded the bundle that lay on her desk.

A present, after ten years, hand-delivered by Corvina beren Oliva herself. Brina emptied the purse Corvina had all but tossed to her. Was bringing the present Corvina's way of disguising the business she had done? Or was the business a distraction from the gift?

Slowly, Mistress Brina untied the bundle, unwrapped it, and held it in her hands.

It was a cordial bottle, cobalt blue, etched with the arms of the House of Sarpa: a lion standing on his hind legs, front claws extended, looking back over his shoulder.

"Shifty beast," the Mistress said. She jiggled the stopper, breaking the red wax seal, and opened the bottle. She sniffed at the bottleneck and at the stopper. "Burnt sugar." Brina capped the bottle again, her eyes unfocused, her fingers twiddling on the desk-top.

For ten years, the old Waymistress had waited, hoping to see Landry over-reach himself, while the Way insisted she accept each day that he did not. Appeasing the House of Sarpa by keeping the last of the House of Onagros under ward had seemed so practical... so simple. If Landry established right of rule, cooperation with him now might buy the Way some tolerance in time to come. If Landry toppled, the House's shelter of the rightful heir of Onagros (renunciation or no renunciation) would glorify the Way in the eyes of the people.

Still, such philosophy in the face of Landry's inferior rule had not been easy. Brina remembered a tale told by the storyteller, Farukh, involving a unicorn, a snake, and indirect deliverance. It would have taken a duller mind than Brina's not to see Layounna in that story, and herself in that unicorn. But what more must she do to wake Sorcha from her lethargy? Flirt with snakebite?

Which brought her thoughts back to her recent visitor. If ever a reptile lived in human form, Corvina was that reptile. Those unicorn stories of Farukh's.... Alicorn and poison made a pair, so often. And Corvina wanted all the Station's alicorn, the same day she asked to give an over-sweet elixir to the throne's true heir.

Well, well, equivocation and semantics assuredly have their uses. Brina went to the cupboard and brought back a large velvet bag and a small one.

Corvina had been told the Station had few pieces of alicorn, had demanded them, and had been sold them. She had not been told that the Station also possessed artifacts made with alicorn; she hadn't asked for them, and so the Station still possessed them.

Brina opened the larger sack and lifted out a chalice, the inner cup inlaid with wafers of alabaster, mother-of-pearl, white marble, and alicorn.

The Waymistress emptied Corvina's phial into the cup. The pieces of alicorn turned an oozy-looking black where the liquid touched them. Within the minute, though, they had regained their milky sheen.

Brina tilted the chalice, so that the liquid touched wafers of alicorn it hadn't touched before. They remained pure. The cordial itself smelled less cloying, and had a clearer look.

The Waymistress lifted the chalice as if to drink from it, but did not drink. Instead, she emptied the cup into a nearby pot of aloe, wiped the cup clean with a cloth, and threw both cloth and cordial bottle into the fire.

"Oh, dear. I seem to have broken Sorcha's lovely gift. At least I can tell her what she's missed through my clumsiness." She emptied the small velvet bag into her palm. A necklace of gold with a pendant gleamed in her hand. The pendant was carved into the shape of a running unicorn, carved from a single piece of shining white. "I'll have to give her this in compensation."

chapter 8
fisherman of the inland sea

Just as the sun was setting, Nerissa topped a small rise and saw stretched before her more water than she would ever have dreamed possible. She had come to the Inland Sea – to the end of her path.

She had long ago given up her fantasy of being the Sea King's daughter. She knew if she threw herself into the water she would only drown. Drowning was something Nerissa was not prepared to do.

Suddenly, she heard the song of her bird. She looked in the direction of the song, but saw only a jumble of stones, each bigger than herself, on a spit of land straight ahead, beyond the path, thrusting into the sea.

She walked around the stones, following the sound, but she found no bird – only rounded boulders and an opening high in the jumble.

The sun on the rocks was pitiless; the strand to her right and the cliffs to her left were equally uninviting. A cool exhalation dropped from the opening and caressed her skin. She clambered up the rocks and crawled in.

The floor of the cave was level, dry, and sandy. She had walked all night and all day; she was too weary even to wonder how she could have done it. Her eyelids drooped. She slept.

When she woke, her den was impenetrably black, but she could hear the crash of waves just under her cave. She felt the waves' foam flung into the opening, tasted the salt.

She knew nothing of tides, but she knew that the sea had risen. Whether it had finished or would rise to fill her shelter and her lungs – that, she did not know.

Now she wept in terror, her tears mingling with the spray on her cheeks.

She heard the sound of birdsong again. Her gleaming guide sat at the mouth of the cave, casting a silver-white light all around it. When she moved toward it, it flew away.

"Don't go!" She crawled to the opening in the rocks.

There, she watched the bird fly higher and higher, growing bigger as it flew instead of smaller, losing its shape as it rose until at last it perched above the earth, a bright full moon. Everything shone softly in its light; the very waves broke more gently and seemed to whisper, "We'll come no nearer. Be easy."

Slap!

A broad, flat hand splayed on the rock near Nerissa's face. She jerked back as the hand tightened and pulled. A coracle edged around the rocks, a small round boat bearing a huge heavy-bodied man. His dark hair was matted and filthy; even his moustache and beard looked tangled. He had a long sinewy neck and a hooked nose so thin-fleshed and bony it gleamed in the moonlight. He grinned with chisel-like teeth and coldly glittering eyes.

"Scared you, didn't I?" he said in a guttural voice. "Come out of that cave; it's mine."

"No!" Nerissa scuttered back as far as she could go. "I won't!"

The man reached in after her, arm stretching, fingers stretching, until he grasped her arm. She beat him with her bony fist and bit at him, but he drew her out of the cave and into the boat.

"Be still or you'll capsize us. I can swim – can you?" The man shook her suddenly, jogging the coracle. Water flapped in and slid around their bare feet.

Nerissa cried out and grasped the man's wrist.

"Answer me, girl. Can you swim?"

"No!"

The man nodded. He shook a long gnarled finger at Nerissa. "To me, you never lie." He picked up a pair of oars and began to row, back the way he had come.

"Who are you?" the girl asked. "Where are you taking me?"

"The name's Tartarus. I'm a fisherman. Saw footprints heading this way and not coming back. You're not the first idiot who's been trapped out there at high tide, and you won't be the last."

"Would the water have come in?"

"Half an hour, and you would have been squid bait."

Nerissa shivered, but the moonlight flashing off the water reminded her of her bird. Her bird, she was certain, wouldn't have left her to drown.

Tartarus, she pointed out to herself, had only said *she* mustn't lie to *him*.

"Give me your name," he said.

"They call me Nerissa."

"Nerissa birn what?"

"Nerissa birn Matka."

After several strokes of his oars, Tartarus said, "You're not from around here."

Nerissa considered not answering, or trying out her imagination on a false history, but she was too conscious of Tartarus' recent warning.

"I'm from Granitz. I'm a slave. I ran away."

Tartarus bellowed a laugh that rang off the rocks behind them. "Good for you, girl! Stole something as you came, did you?"

"A few coppers. Myself. Nothing much."

Tartarus shrugged, as if he were resigned to disappointment in his fellow creatures.

The coracle rasped against sand. Tartarus got out and pulled the boat, with Nerissa in it, out of the water. He hauled it across the sand, over a hummock, and into an overhung pocket of sandy rock. He lifted Nerissa out and set her on her feet, neither winded nor sweating from his labor.

While Nerissa was still trying to decide whether or not to run, the huge man squatted before her, holding up that cautionary finger.

"You owe me one day's service for that rescue. My hut's just yonder; can you clean and cook?"

"I did what cleaning and cooking there was at home. I'm not very good at either of them, though."

Tartarus nodded. "You'll do. I'm not dainty. If it suits you and if it suits me, you can stay. We'll just have to see."

Nerissa found walking in the sand a bit difficult at first, but her companion moved slowly enough for her to keep up. He was dressed in short pants of some coarse cloth, and a sleeveless shirt that was little more than a baggy vest. He was barefoot; his feet were as broad and flat as his hands.

She looked away from the sand and into the sky. The stars were clear and brilliant, but so far away. Even the moon – the moon her bird had become – shone with only the promise of companionship, not the reality.

Tartarus was real – ugly, dirty, unpleasant, with nothing to offer but thankless work. This was like walking on solid ground to Nerissa. This was like waking from a floating dream and finding herself bound to the hard earth again. In a way, it was welcome. It was normal. It was no more than she could expect.

Tartarus led her up a rocky slope to a hut tucked into a shelf of the seaside cliff.

"Nice and private," he said, opening the shabby door.

Nerissa hesitated in the doorway while Tartarus lit a lamp.

The hut was small – smaller than the room she had shared with Barand and Isa. It was really a lean-to, the back wall being the cliff's bare rock, where a hole at the bottom of a natural chimney served as a fireplace. There were no windows. Nerissa saw a pile of cloth in a corner and a lamp hanging from the ceiling, a set of shelves knocked out of the stone wall and filled with dented pots and pans, and a rummage of wooden dishes and utensils. A broom leaned against one of the wooden walls, cobwebs fastening it in place.

No, Tartarus wasn't dainty, Nerissa thought.

"Come in, girl. Aren't you afraid of the dark? Don't you know Tortoise comes after bad little runaway slaves at night?"

Nerissa snorted contemptuously and folded her arms, standing just outside the open doorway.

"That old story doesn't scare me anymore."

Tartarus sneered. "Ah, but it used to, didn't it? I've heard some versions that scared *me*, I'll tell you. Mind you, it's nonsense, isn't it? Bound to be."

Nerissa came in, then, and closed the door.

Tartarus tossed her an armful of rags. "Make yourself a bed somewhere. I like mine over here." He kicked another bundle of rags into a heap against the left-hand wall.

Nerissa opened and folded the cloths, putting the thickest on the bottom and wrapping herself in the thinnest. She lay down as Tartarus blew out the lamp. The last thing she saw was the glow of the lamp's dying wick reflected off the curve of Tartarus' nose. The last thing she heard was his guttural voice, saying, "If Tortoise took bites out of anybody, it would be *good* little children."

chapter 9
mortal blood

Corvina beren Oliva guided her dun-colored mare across the Kudasad Bridge. Four villeins from the castle walked – one ahead, one behind, and one on each side – protecting the Kinninger's sister from the contamination of a commoner's touch. Corvina was not unaware of the covert looks that followed her; she knew her brother's people would love to touch her – with sticks and rocks and mud.

Landry is a fool. If I controlled the realm, these churls would be casting their cloaks in my path to protect my horse's hooves from dirt.

As always, her musings were clear about the people's adulation, but vague on the means by which she would achieve it. She believed, though, that the purchase she had just made at the Waystation was an important step toward her desire.

She had wanted alicorn because she knew that Rhu beren Robia, the Chamberlain, had been sent hunting unicorns and that the hunt was Oliva's idea. Anything Oliva prized was worth the having. So she had gone on a hunt of her own, and had succeeded where the man had failed. At least she was bringing back *something*, when he had returned empty-handed.

Just what had prompted the hunt, she had not been told. She was an alchemist, a follower of the writings of the Great Adept, Tarkastrus; she knew the legendary powers of a unicorn's body. She also knew the value her mother, as an adept in Tarkastrian ritual worship, would place on so powerful a sacrifice. Although it fell far short of a living unicorn, perhaps this offering of hers would gain Oliva's confidences.

Brina's box nestled safely within her bodice. Nestled and chafed – chafed and burned. The seemingly smooth surface must have been riddled with tiny splinters, which were now making themselves apparent. The irritating heat spread as Corvina rode, to her fingers, to her toes, to her head.

The sun was oppressive. Corvina drew her light cape's hood to shield her face, but now she found it difficult to breathe.

At last she could dismount and, leaving her horse for a stable-boy to tend, take refuge in the castle.

The air in the kitchen hall seemed stale. She clawed off her cape and let it drop behind her on the stairs down to her workroom. The steps seemed steeper and less regular than she remembered them being.

She stumbled into her retreat and dragged her purchase from its place of safety. The source of torment shifted from her breastbone to her hand. By the time she realized her misery came from the alicorn, the unassuming little box rolled from her hand and she sank to the stones.

"Moder." She felt her lips form the word.

And Oliva, in her tower room, heard and came to her.

~*~

"Are you better, my child?"

Oliva beren Audre's voice was tender – anxious. She perched on the edge of Corvina's bed, her tiny figure hardly pressing the mattress. She held one of Corvina's hands. She rubbed the knuckles of her other hand gently over her daughter's cheek, in a nursery gesture of comfort.

Tears prickled Corvina's eyes, surprising both women.

Corvina pulled her hand and face away from her mother and said, with a look of sickly fear, "You'd better not. Better not touch me."

Oliva's lips twitched, suppressing a smile that would insult Corvina's solicitude. "No danger to me, child."

"But you don't know. I had no chance to tell you...."

"I found you in your workroom, on the floor, in riding clothes. I found a pillbox near your hand."

"What did you do with it?"

"I left it where I found it." She laid two fingers softly on the bodice of Corvina's nightgown.

Corvina winced.

"There's a swollen bruise there," said Oliva. "The size and shape of a pillbox. You didn't fall on the box; that would have crushed it." Oliva leaned forward. "What happened?"

"The box is yours. I bought its contents from old Brina, the Waymistress."

"And what does it contain?"

"Haven't you looked?"

"At something from your workroom? Something near you, and you insensible? Who taught you caution?"

Corvina smiled. "You. It seems I have much to learn yet."

"What have you brought me that's done this to you?"

Corvina narrowed her eyes. "Are we alone?"

"We are."

"Did you lock my workroom door?"

"I locked it while I went for help, stood inside while the villeins carried you out, and locked it again behind us. Whatever you brought is safe." She looked again at her daughter's limp hair, normally shining in soft tight curls, at her sallow face, rose-flushed olive only this morning, at her sunken eyes, their rich mahogany dull and flat. "It's secure, at any rate."

Corvina whispered, "Alicorn."

"The Waymistress! How did you ever think to ask the Waymistress?"

"Rumors through my sources. It was a hope...a bluff that worked."

"And you've brought it to me?"

"Yes.... But Moder.... That box is death."

"I understand. Corvina, you must never handle alicorn, nor anything that ever lived that holds it. Stone can contain it for you, or metal, but never wood or cloth."

"Take it. You wanted it for something, and wouldn't tell me what. Now you have it."

Oliva raised Corvina's hands and kissed them. "My precious girl." She held the hands tightly, against her own slight body. "I wouldn't have exchanged your life for it. Not for an entire unicorn, alive." The last female of the House of Sarpa; no, Corvina was not expendable. "Shall I tell you why I wanted alicorn?"

Corvina nodded.

"Landry and I have made a mandate bag. It wanted only this. Alicorn, for the right to rule." Oliva's eyes shone. "You've given our House legitimacy. Landry can reign unopposed."

"In the name of beren Ada!"

"In the name of beren Oliva. With this bag, he no longer needs to cling to Karol's name. He can set it aside, and hold the throne for Sarpa."

"And what does that do for us?"

"It places our line on the throne."

"What line? Landry has no heirs, and never will."

"He's young –"

"He never will."

"Corvina...." Oliva released her daughter's hands.

Corvina laughed the word, "No!" She shook her head, her blue-black hair rustling on the pillow. "It's none of my doing. I'm not that ambitious! If I were, I'd have dealt with Hayward's brood; there's where the line would have led."

"Hayward's children are half Onagros."

"And their names are beren Sorcha, not beren Oliva. But what I meant was: What woman would breed with Landry?"

"Corvina!"

"Any woman who would trust herself to him, *I* wouldn't trust."

"You're speaking of your Kinninger!"

"I'm speaking of my brother."

She half-expected her mother to take offense, but Oliva permitted herself to show a small curl of a smile.

Corvina went on: "How deeply are you in his counsels? Shall I tell you what really took me to the Waystation? The errand I undertook to cover my search for the alicorn? I went for Landry. Did you know that?"

Oliva lifted her chin and swiveled her head toward the door, as if her gaze could travel through the thick wood and into Landry's part of the castle.

"He didn't tell you, did he?" Corvina asked. "He didn't think I'd tell you, either. He gave me no chance, before I left, but I'll not keep his secrets from you –"

"What have you done?"

"He sent me with a present for Sorcha. A cordial of my own making."

"A cordial?"

"Sweet," said Corvina, "and deadly."

Oliva nodded, her mouth pursed. Landry wanted Sorcha dead. That was sensible, though hardly necessary. He wanted Sorcha dead by someone's hand, other than his own. That, too, was sensible. But to place his own sister in the way of any retribution that might result – that was unforgivable.

"You may be in danger," she said. "The people have a strong fondness for Sorcha. If she dies, Brina will make it widely known Landry sent you –"

"A fact I made quite clear. Brina has a reputation for cleverness; with luck, my brother's gift will be destroyed unopened. If the Waymistress is stupid enough – or frightened enough – to actually deliver it, she'll be complicit, and we'll have nothing to fear from her."

"He should not have risked…. He should have consulted me."

"He didn't want advice. He tried to flatter me that I was being consulted, but I know a request from an order. Don't you understand him yet, Moder? The House of Sarpa doesn't mean the line to Landry; it means himself. He drove Hayward's wife and children into namelessness and exile; now he wants Sorcha dead – just to make sure, I suppose. Hayward will never remarry, if he hasn't yet. And Landry will have no heirs."

"Aha," said Oliva. "So that leaves only you, is that it?"

"Frankly, yes. I'm glad I got the alicorn. I'm glad to give it to you. Let Landry claim the throne legitimately for us. I lack your gift for prophecy, but I predict it will be my children who hold that throne."

"Yours?"

"Ahh," Corvina raised a finger. "You see, I have several things to offer that Landry can't. First, I see myself as one bead on our family's chain, not a pendant that the chain was made to serve. Second, I can assure my fertility." She held up a hand to forestall her mother's question, "– Yes, and the health of my issue, as well." Corvina's expression grew no grimmer than her mother's as she said, "My lost child, Moder, died by the hand of my husband. By the hand of my late husband. I am older, now, and wiser. Any future husband who threatens me or mine will not last as long as my first."

Oliva tucked the coverlet more closely around her daughter.

Corvina returned to her listing: "My third recommendation is that my children will bear my matronym, and my first-born girl will be named Oliva – Oliva beren Corvina – and her heir will be Corvina beren Oliva. We can see to it, by decree or by tradition, that there is always an Oliva or a beren Oliva of the House of Sarpa on the throne."

And, Oliva thought, *by the same token, always a Corvina or a beren Corvina.*

"Fourth, I serve Tarkastrus as faithfully as you do. And, fifth…I can take a useful man for my husband."

"What useful man do you favor?"

"A landed Thane. A man other men follow, even into death. Lowborn, but highly favored now."

"Guthrie beren Melanell?" Oliva laughed harshly. "You would marry the Chief of your brother's Swords? Does your taste run that way?"

"My taste is not under consideration. You and I have been thrust away from power along with all other women. There are only two men close to Landry, both much closer than either of us. One is Thane Guthrie. The other is the Chamberlain. My taste isn't for either of them, but at least Guthrie has the advantages I named – and blood in his veins, instead of chilly water. Or does Rhu the Chamberlain please you more? Would you prefer I take a family servant for my husband?"

Oliva's sour expression answered for her.

"I'm only speaking of a husband, after all," Corvina said. "I can choose someone more suitable to father my children."

"True. But I wonder if Guthrie would be content to marry in name only."

"Content or not, he'll do as we tell him. Oh, we'll couch it as an honor – perhaps you could propose the match to Landry and Landry could offer it to him. I could pretend to protest, then give in. Landry would like that."

Oliva shook her head, a frown on her forehead, a smile touching her lips. Then she thought more deeply about Thane Guthrie and the smile evaporated. "That man has a secret – not one of Landry's, but one of his own. He's very near to bringing it to me, I think. I'd like to know it before this plan proceeds."

Corvina's face slackened suddenly, and she groaned as if wrung with painful weariness. "Moder…." She licked her dry lips. "I'm not dying, am I?"

Oliva patted her daughter's hand. "No, no, my dear. You've just been weakened. I've brought you something from your workroom, and there's hot water here. A tonic will do you good."

She helped Corvina sit up and handed her a stone goblet with a dusting of powder in the bottom.

"What is it?" Corvina asked.

"It was labeled 'nightshade.' That should pick you up."

"Nightshade is poison." Corvina watched her mother fetch water from the hearth.

"So it is," said Oliva.

Corvina held out the goblet. Oliva poured the steaming water into the cup and replaced the kettle on the stones.

"How long have you known?" Corvina asked.

"It's common for alchemists to… desensitize themselves to the harmful effects of certain elements of their compounds. The alicorn was drawing the poison from your body. Since your body is filled with poison, it was leeching your very life."

"I should have realized."

The women smiled at one another. Corvina drank her tonic.

Oliva left Corvina a little strengthened and returned to the cellar workroom. The box was where it had fallen, on its side on the floor.

She picked up the box, listening to the quiet click of its contents. She opened it and drew a sharp breath. The alicorn chips shone. They could be no more than a century old – perhaps less. No wonder they had acted so quickly and so powerfully. Oliva turned the chips out onto her palm, letting the torchlight play over their opalescent surface. This was a fortune: two chips of freshest alicorn. One for Landry's mandate bag… and one for Landry's mother.

Corvina congratulated herself on having at least a scrap of instinct. Stone or metal, her mother had said, would safely contain alicorn for an alchemist. She had shaken one chip into a tiny stone mortar before her collapse.

She didn't regret giving her mother the other chips. The mandate bag was a stroke of genius on her mother's part. The alicorn would make the difference between an empty symbol and an object of real power, and Corvina had provided it. That made the mandate hers, as far as she was concerned.

"How is Corvina? What ails her?"

Oliva had been summoned to Landry's rooms while she had been dressing for dinner.

Landry, Oliva thought, achingly. *Such a beautiful boy….* Still slender as a youth, his full black hair now twisted into an elongated knot down the back of his neck, he was still her prettiest child, with her own coloring and his lamented father's height. But it wasn't looks that mattered now, it was family feeling. If Landry were truly lacking in it, he was Oliva's child no more.

"Corvina is well enough. Will your Grace permit an old woman to sit down?"

Landry flapped a hand toward the hearth-side chairs. Oliva lowered herself into one. Landry, either unaware of Oliva's helpless act or unaffected by it, perched on the edge of the facing chair.

"What happened to Corvina?" Landry asked.

"Suppose you tell me."

Landry sat back, blinking. "What do you mean?"

"I think you know. More than you pretend, at any rate. – I see that sulky look in your eyes, My Lord; Corvina didn't carry tales to me. I had the story out of her in her illness and weakness. Landry… my dear, what were you thinking? You're not a fool or a coward. Why did you set your sister to murder an inoffensive nobody who could only be dangerous murdered?"

"Are you deaf, Moder? Don't you hear the stories and rumors my agents bring me every day?"

"If I hear anything, it isn't from your telling me!" Oliva snapped. "Your confidence, you save for another."

One corner of Landry's mouth twisted upward. "Jealous of a peasant?"

"I am. When my son rejects the guidance he can trust the most for a self-serving upstart – Indeed I am jealous, My Lord!"

"Well, then, you know what I've done. Someone who goes into cloister could come out."

"And if your plan miscarries? If she doesn't take the bait? If she lives, and knows you tried to kill her?"

"Let her take it as a warning. Let all who oppose me take it as a warning."

"Landry, none will dare oppose you after Midsummer Day. Who could oppose you, now? I tell you, no one with a right to claim it wants the throne. You have no children and need have none, if you want none. Your brother's children are disinherited by both their parents; they might never have been born. Corvina's are in the future and they'll be sworn to your service. Or do you doubt Corvina?" This was the vital question.

"Corvina…. What happened to her, Moder? I never meant anything to happen to her."

"She was on your business. More wholeheartedly than you knew, my son. See what she brought you, at peril of her life."

Oliva took the pillbox from her girdle and handed it to Landry. He opened it and picked the chip from it.

"Is it…?"

"Alicorn. New, for a new royal line. Strong, for a strong one. But we won't be strong if we're at cross-purposes. Your sister and I are your most devoted servants, my darling boy. Why, Corvina has refrained from choosing a second husband; even this basic right, she places at your disposal."

"Does she?" Landry looked thoughtful, turning the alicorn in his fingers. "I wonder…. Would she place her children in foster care for me? Would she hide their true birth from them if I asked it, and only have them told on my death or by my wish?"

"Yes."

"Would she hide them from me, as Karol did?"

"Would it do her more good than it did Karol?"

Landry raised his head very slowly, and met his mother's eyes with a gaze more direct than he'd given her since his childhood.

"Karol's children would now be at my side or on my lap, if they had also been mine. Don't mistake me, Moder. I don't fear what's mine, and I don't protect myself from what I don't fear. I love Corvina but – trust her?"

"If you want your own child on the throne, you'd best beget one. Corvina wants a part in the succession – as do I, my dear – but it seems the only part either of us will ever have is raising the successors."

Landry leaned forward and took Oliva's fisted hand.

"Is that so bitter to you both?"

"It isn't natural! Where are the women at your court? In the shadows, if anywhere! When one segment of the body outgrows the rest, physicians call it 'diseased' and try to cure it."

The Kinninger smiled and gave Oliva's hand a little shake. "I can control the men. Women are beyond me. So, again, I protect myself."

"Then you need me. Can't you see how well Corvina and I could serve you? What do you think we'll do, your sister and I? Lead a coup against you? To what purpose?"

"To gain power–"

"Which we'd have, if you chose to restore it to us. Who would I place on the throne but you?"

"Yourself."

Oliva spread her hands in appeal. "I gave you the running of Sarpa before your marriage. If I didn't covet administering my own lands, why would I want the burden of a country?"

"Corvina," Landry said.

Oliva laughed. "Corvina, indeed! I won't say she hasn't dreamed of it, though I don't know she has. Corvina is no fool, but she has no head for administrative details. She's a proud woman, as befits a sister of yours; she resents being the youngest and chafes at your belittling of her – as a child and now. Would you have her submit meekly, like that Elsie person who came and went like the nothing she was? That is not the way of a Sarpan."

After a brief silence, Landry said, "Who would she marry?"

Oliva suppressed a triumphant smile and said, "If you ask who she favors, I couldn't say. If you ask who she'd take, I'd say she'd take anyone you choose – both for husband and for child-sire."

"Yes." Landry sat back with a quirk at his lips. "They needn't be the same."

The silence fermented again while Landry considered his mother's counsel. He had done well enough without it – well enough for long enough to prove he didn't really need it. Perhaps the time had come to return his mother to a place of some importance. Perhaps it would strengthen his position now rather than weaken it. And perhaps Corvina would be more comfortable as an ally than as a rival.

Thane Oliva hoped her relief was hidden. Her sons had grown so far away from her she hardly knew what to expect from them. At the beginning of this interview, she had thought it credible that Landry might be a mortal threat to his sister and even to herself. Now, she knew that he was not – certainly not unless he saw clear proof of danger to himself from them, possibly not then. Now she knew that Corvina had been wrong about Landry's estimation of his House and his place in it.

"Would she take…Thane Guthrie?" Landry asked, his own distaste obvious.

Now that the possibility was real, Oliva recoiled from it with a sound very near a grunt. "If that is your wish, I believe she would. As husband, I trust you mean, not as father of your heirs."

"Well, naturally. My Chief of Swords is becoming restless again; I'm running out of honors to toss him, to keep him more-or-less content. Perhaps marriage into the royal family would be unusually effective."

"Three feet of steel in the hands of his Lieutenant would be more effective, still."

Landry gasped, and laughed until the tears sprang from the corners of his eyes. "You're blunt, when you feel sure of yourself. I had forgotten that.

I had even forgotten how much I've missed it. – Yes, it would be effective, but it would also rob me of a man who may be useful to me alive for some years yet. He's done things and knows things…. You know that, Moder. Someday, those assets will be liabilities. For now, I need him."

"Something torments him. Something that has nothing to do with you, or only marginally. We must know what it is before we give him my name. Send him to me and invite him to speak freely. He may be longing for a chance to let it out. If I can help – and if I think my helping him is helping you – I will. Even if I can't, anything I learn would be useful, would it not?"

"Perhaps. Perhaps."

Landry curled his hand around the alicorn and thumped the arm of his chair. "Well, then. I'll send Guthrie to you. Do what you can with him and let me know what you think. If it seems advisable to you, broach the match to Corvina. If she's willing, we'll schedule the wedding for after Midsummer Day. You and Corvina will return to the councils. Work your way in slowly, to give my men time to reaccustom themselves to giving your words the weight they deserve. You and Corvina and I will choose the proper scion for our line; where and how the children are reared, we'll decide when the time comes. Are we agreed?"

Oliva patted her older son's cheek, the familiar gesture feeling rather awkward after all this time. "Agreed."

~*~

That night, Oliva beren Audre bound her chip of alicorn to her forehead with a cloth of undyed silk, drank a potion of wine mixed with powdered blood, and slept.

She dreamed of drinking blood from a fountain, steam rising from it like spray. She was a silver-gray lady, slim as a knife and cold as a corpse. She burned with cold. She ached. She felt as if she were chained by the soul. She held her hands up to the fountain, let it cascade over her and felt a little peace. A man's hand encircled her throat and clutched her, pulled her back from her pleasure. His hand trembled but he choked her, still.

The man was Guthrie. He looked at her with hatred. He drew her close and held her tightly. "Sing to me," he whispered. "Serve me. Let me be."

Then he stood, sword drawn, by a river, a bridle with a silver bit glinting at his waist. The sword was aflame. Guthrie's hand clutched it as it burned. His face was agonized. The muscles of his arm corded and jumped with the effort of holding on, the refusal to let go. A shining creature swam across the river, not far from him. It turned its head and Oliva saw it was a unicorn. It struggled to move away, but approached Guthrie as if drawn to him. Guthrie took a step, plunged his flaming sword hilt-deep into the shining body, and drew it out. Water gushed from the murdered unicorn, quenching the flame, bathing the man in freedom.

~*~

"Welcome, my fellow Thane. Thank you for coming."

Guthrie beren Melanell entered Oliva's room and turned, startled, as Oliva's body servant slipped out, closing the door behind her.

"We'll be more comfortable alone," said Oliva. "Come sit by me."

"Yes....All right." Thane Guthrie seemed ill at ease, his hands fluttering like hawks with no place to roost.

"Will you pour us some wine?"

Guthrie did as he was asked, gratefully. The action gave him something to do; the glass, something to handle. He sat in the chair across from Oliva, glancing at his left side and shifting uncomfortably.

"Thank you for leaving your sword elsewhere. You feel odd without her, I imagine."

"Yes."

"Free?"

"No."

"Because you know she's still there. Waiting for you." Oliva leaned forward suddenly and put a tiny hand on one of Guthrie's. She really did feel pity for him, after that dream. That time he'd nearly confided in her shortly after Landry's ascension he had shown the signs of a man in spiritual torment. Since then, he had seemed to find his balance. Now, after her dream, now that she knew to look again, Oliva could see that his balance was dearly held.

Guthrie filled the chair across from her. He seemed both too solid, as if his weight were heavy with lifelessness, and insubstantial, as if his most essential part were missing. His rusty hair was cut short – on his head, on his upper lip, on the sides of his face – as if he couldn't spare the energy to let it grow. His green eyes were like tree snakes, still and dangerous.

"You have a name for your sword, I believe?"

"Deya beren Blotha, My Lady."

"Death, born of Blood. Your mistress is well-named."

Guthrie jerked, spilling wine over his hand and Oliva's.

"I dreamed of you last night," she said. "I dreamed of both of you." Oliva leaned farther forward, as if sharing a secret that might be overheard. "I dreamed of your deliverance."

Guthrie whispered, "How?"

"The Chamberlain has failed us. He found no unicorn; claimed there was none to be found. I believe differently."

"Has he dared to betray the throne –" Guthrie sought his sword, fumbling at her absence.

"Not deliberately. He lacks the mettle for that." Oliva smiled a self-congratulatory smile; it wasn't easy to break a spirit, yet leave it useful. "I think he's been the unwitting tool of another force, at odds with mine."

"What other force? What does that have to do with…? What does that have to do with me?"

"Where did you get that sword?"

"She comes from Kozabir. I killed a man in the Northern Border War and took her from him."

"Kozabir…. Yes, of course. – Listen, then: My dream tells me that you may take, by compulsion, what the Chamberlain could not take by persuasion. The domination that sword wields over you can only be broken by one thing: the blood of a unicorn."

"You said before I'd never catch a unicorn."

"My dream has shown me a way. I want the beast alive, but I no longer ask for that. Bringing the beast to me alive and in secret would be the most impressive feat you ever managed."

"Would it?" Guthrie remembered another quite impressive feat. He still dreamed of the sea of blood, of the cries of lost children.

"It would. However, if you cannot capture it, you must kill it. Quickly and cleanly, with one blow. Do you understand?"

Guthrie nodded.

"Now, you must go to Kozabir – to Granitz. Show your sword. Surely a man who makes such things will be known to someone. Find him. Bring him here. I want him under my eye while he works."

"Works at what, My Lady?"

"A bridle, all of silver and silk, filled with the kind of power that fills your sword. Bait, to catch a unicorn. The beauty and power of such a bridle will lure the beast to you. If you can slip the bit into its mouth, if you can bring it to me alive, you will dispatch it for me. Only I have presided in my temple, but you shall be Priest and I your acolyte." When she looked into Guthrie's green eyes, she could see him garbed in emerald, soaked in scarlet. "If the creature is too wary to take the bit, hang the bridle from a tree and wait. When it comes to inspect the enchantment – strike!"

"Quickly and cleanly," said Guthrie, as if in a dream. "With one blow."

"I have no detailed accounts of the slaying of a unicorn, but piecing together what I do have I think you can expect this: the flesh will decay; at the same time, the blood will turn to powder. Whether there will be a noxious fume, I cannot say. If you see any smoke or color in the air, stand away, as you value your life. When all is through, you should be left with a skinful of bones and dried blood. Fold the head back on the body and roll it up carefully, keeping the horn in place and taking care not to pierce the hide."

Better, Oliva thought, not to tell Guthrie of the ruby said to be at the base of the horn. The man wasn't fool enough to try to pocket something Oliva meant for her own, but temptation was better kept out of a servant's way.

"I'll give you a silken cloth and a canvas bag to wrap and carry the remains. When you've stored it all away, wash yourself thoroughly. Leave nothing on your body or your clothes and, whatever you do, get nothing in your mouth, on your lips, or in your eyes. Do you understand that?"

"No, My Lady, but I'll do as you say."

Now, Oliva thought, *for the bait to catch a Sword.*

"I have another proposition for you, Thane Guthrie."

"Yes, My Lady?"

"Thane Guthrie…," Oliva could hardly bring herself to say the words: "have you never married?"

"No time, My Lady. No inclination."

"Marriage need not be a matter of inclination. People of our class marry for practical reasons." Oliva hoped the Chief Sword didn't hear the sarcasm she detected in her own voice as she said the words "*our* class."

"Who would I marry? May I ask you to advise me?"

It amused Oliva, touched her, gave her a slightly higher opinion of Guthrie, this proof that his ambition had never presumed to consider the connection she was about to propose.

"Corvina," she said, and watched Guthrie's face change from incredulity to caution.

"I don't deserve such an honor. How can you suggest such a match?"

"Corvina's a strong woman. You're a stronger man. Corvina's been unmarried far too long. Her first husband, you may know, mistreated her. She lost a daughter to his brutality. Corvina swore never to marry again."

"Why now? Why me?"

"My son, His Grace, wishes it."

"He does?"

"I told you he valued you. What better way to show it than by allying his blood with yours?"

Oliva could almost hear Guthrie telling himself how he would produce heirs from Corvina, how Landry's death would put Corvina or her heirs on the throne, and how easy it would be to take that final step to the throne, himself.

Oliva, on the other hand, trusted to Corvina's elixirs to prevent any heirs of Guthrie's making. And, if push came to shove, Corvina had as much as said she would find a second widowhood as bearable as her first, and as easily achieved.

"Will you consider the match?" said Oliva.

"I will. I mean, I accept. I mean, I thank you, My Lady, for counting me worthy."

"Be a good husband to my daughter, a good vassal to my son, and a good friend to me. If you accept our proposal, the marriage ceremonies will take place after Midsummer Day. I depend on you, Thane Guthrie."

Now, Oliva thought, *weave what dreams you will from that.*

chapter 10
ENCOUNTER IN The RAIN

Now that events were moving, Kinnan was content to linger, to progress carefully through the Geiskeflor into the Fiddlewood. Barely out of sight and sound of the smithy, he stopped and turned, scanning the path behind.

"Forget something?" Brady asked.

Kinnan shook his head. "If your Elsie got this far, this is the way she would face. I have to see what she'd see to find where she might shelter."

"So...you're going to walk to Pazni backward?"

Kinnan scowled. "Are you mocking your own quest?"

"No, no. That would be just like me, but I'm not. I don't know how a soldier searches a forest."

"We'll walk, and every so often I'll stop and scan what Elsie would have seen."

When Kinnan turned to walk on, Brady blocked the way, demanding truth.

"We can't search every bush and hollow for...bones and...and scraps of cloth. What are our chances of finding...anything?"

"We don't think about that. We just look."

Their progress was slow and nearly silent until they camped for the night. They didn't need a fire; Trahern's "useful" cooking pot provided a stew of pork and turnips. Brady built a fire, anyway.

"For the cheerfulness of it," he said, but Kinnan suspected that motive. He knew enough of hope against odds to understand that Brady built the fire not to cheer himself, but to draw a living Elsie back to safety.

Hoping to distract him, Kinnan spoke of Kozabir, finding and comparing places, food, and customs they both knew. It was the surface camaraderie of soldiers' camps, familiar to Kinnan but halting and awkward for Brady, who was more accustomed to masking details than exploring them. When Kinnan fell silent, Brady played his pipes, a tune of airy sweetness that made the Layounnan want to weep.

~*~

The next day dawned cloudy and grew darker by the hour. Their path passed through some thickets so dense they needed Trahern's lantern for its ordinary light.

By afternoon, they heard a light rain on the canopy of leaves, but only an occasional drop found its way through to the forest floor. The rain increased, and so did the leakage. When the path and the river had run parallel for several hours, a rumble of thunder split the clouds and nothing short of four walls and a roof could have kept the travelers dry.

"It could be worse," shouted Brady, the words bubbling through the sheet of rain that had just blown into his face. "We still have a little daylight – if you can call this 'daylight.'"

Water hissed on millions of leaves and twigs, and clattered in millions of accumulated patterings onto the forest floor. It beat the surface of the Fiddlewood River into a rippled leaden gleam, barely visible through the downpour and the intervening trees.

"Why don't you turn yourself into something that doesn't mind the wet?" Kinnan shouted back. "No sense in both of us being soaked."

"Too late, now. Just as well to find shelter and dry out together."

The scream of a horse, full of fury and frustration, shocked Brady to silence, and both men staggered to a halt.

"What was that?" said Brady.

Kinnan put his lips close to Brady's ear and said, "Be still. That sounded like a war horse."

"In the Fiddlewood? In this weather?"

"That's why I say, 'Be still.' Only someone under orders would ride here on a day like this. Stay here or follow quietly."

"Follow where?"

"I need to see –"

Brady clutched Kinnan's sodden travel cloak to bring his ear back into range. "You don't need to see, you only need to know. Let me look. I can do it safely."

Kinnan nodded. He pointed ahead and toward the river. "It came from that direction."

Brady disappeared. A chameleon wriggled off the path and flashed over the forest floor. Perversely, the rain slackened as soon as the boy was waterproof.

A moment later, there were two more screams: another from the horse, and one from something else.

"Brady!" Kinnan loosened his sword and started toward the sounds. He heard Brady: "Kinnan! *This way*! HURRY!"

Kinnan pushed through a mass of leafy seedlings and almost knocked Brady to his knees.

"Up there!" Brady pointed, face raised into the slanting rain.

But Kinnan couldn't look up. Not right away. First he had to look at what stood before him.

It was twice the size of a war horse – huge and black – the rain careening off the mass of it and falling again in torrents around it. Its mane, a different shade of black, ran like darker water down its trunk-like neck. Its hooves were mired in the muddy detritus of the riverbank. Its head was lowered, its forehead facing a tree, its nose pointing toward the ground. As Kinnan watched, it shook its head and the tree trembled.

"Up there!" Brady threw something and that second scream sounded again.

Kinnan looked up. A mountain lion crouched in a crook of the tree, ears back, face contorted in a snarl of rage.

Brady picked up another rock.

"Lions don't hunt in the rain," Kinnan said.

"Do you hear that?" Brady shouted. "Lions don't hunt in the rain." He ran toward the lion's tree. He threw his rock and picked up another.

"Leave it alone! You can't drive it off – you'll just draw its attack!"

The warning came too late. The cougar gathered itself and leaped over the gigantic horse. It landed where Brady had stood, but it landed in the arms of a bear, knocking him to the ground with its momentum. As a bear, thick fur protected Brady from the cougar's claws and teeth, but he found that what had impressed two farmers and a dog did not impress a cougar.

Brady clutched his attacker in the bear's powerful arms and rolled over on it, roaring for help.

"I can't go *through* you!" Kinnan cried.

The cougar suddenly found itself belly-up and breathless, with a chameleon scuttling off its chest to take cover under a nearby bush.

Kinnan drew his sword but wasn't quick enough to strike. The cougar shook its head and rolled into a crouch. Kinnan braced himself to meet its attack. He wanted to do as little footwork on that treacherous ground as possible.

The cougar leapt. Kinnan met it with the point of his sword, leaning into it. He had misjudged the lion's arc, or the pounding rain had subtly altered it, or the bear's mauling had taken some toll on the creature's muscles, for the leap was short. The edge of the sword slid through the lion's shoulder, and one of its oversized paws connected with the side of Kinnan's head.

Kinnan whirled and fell as the big cat's claws raked his scalp. He lay helpless, partially stunned by the blow on one side of his head and rough ground on the other. The lion's interrupted leap carried it into the river. With a final snarl, it was caught in the current and swept away.

There was a splintering sound and a changed pattern of rainfall. Kinnan realized he had closed his eyes, and fought to open them.

Brady rattled through the underbrush, talking as he came: "He went under just around this bend. I think he's done for." He stumbled over the fallen man. "*No!*" He knelt and turned Kinnan onto his back, leaning over him to shelter his face from the rain.

Kinnan opened his eyes. "Help me sit. Where's my sword?"

Brady levered him up against a clump of roots and retrieved the sword. He dropped it. Gingerly, he picked it up again.

"What's the matter?"

With a troubled look, Brady said, "Nothing. The sword.... I think it has some power in it."

Kinnan smiled. "Trahern made it, after all."

"Yes, but – Look!" Brady pointed to the bank.

The massive horse was gone. The mud that had held its feet was churned into a morass. The trunk of the tree it had faced was torn; sap colored the edges of the gash.

"Lightning?" said Kinnan.

"*It* must have done it, when it pulled away."

"How?"

"It worked its way free."

"Yes, from the mud," said Kinnan. "But what happened to the tree?"

"It left that hole when it pulled out its horn," Brady explained, with the attitude of a man stating the obvious. He looked more closely at his companion. "Are you sure you're all right? Are you dizzy?"

Kinnan put his hand to his head where the lion had struck him. "How bad is it? Is it bleeding?"

"Hard to tell. It washes off as quickly as it comes out. Doesn't seem to be very deep… but… yes… it's bleeding."

"We'll have to find shelter. – Did you say, 'When it pulled out its horn'?"

"It was a unicorn. Didn't you see it?"

"It was a war horse."

"A horse? *That?*"

"Help me up. Help me over to that tree."

"What are you looking for?" Brady asked, as Kinnan draped himself against the trunk, his eyes close to the gouge in the wood.

"This." Kinnan picked something out of the oozing sap. "And this." He showed it to Brady. Pinched between his strong slender fingers were two curls of something striped black and white, as fine as sewing thread, as stiff as wood shavings. "Alicorn. Stripped off when it freed itself – held in the sap." He unbuttoned a pocket, tucked the shavings into it, and buttoned it again. "This is a priceless treasure. You don't know what this means to me, in my position."

"Tell me later. I think I saw a light from around there, to the south." Brady made himself larger than Kinnan and bulged his muscles. "Put an arm around my neck."

"I'm all right now. I can walk."

"Do what I say, or I'll get bigger and carry you."

It nearly came to that, after all. Kinnan was dizzy and weak, and he thought he felt a faint warmth from the sheath at his side, a faint satisfied hum from something both inside and outside himself.

"There it is! Just a glint. Did you see it?"

"That's on the other side of the river. I can walk, but I can't swim."

"There's a causeway here; the water barely covers it."

They stood before the door of a low stone hut.

Brady returned to his proper shape slowly, with his teeth and fists clenched. He relaxed into himself, pale with dismay. "I changed back."

"You had a hard time of it, didn't you?"

"…I was trying *not* to."

Brady retreated a step as the door swung open. His instinct was to slip away – he could almost hear an inner voice prodding him to run. Only Kinnan's inability to run along with him kept him where he was.

A tall, stocky old woman, leaning lightly on a cane, stood silhouetted by the cottage fire.

"Come in, Young Master," she said. "You're wetter than I am. Come in, and your young friend with you."

She put out a hand that glistened pale in the splashing rain and drew Kinnan into the hut.

Brady followed, slightly giddy from his shape-changing tug-of-war.

"Bring more flannels!" the old woman called. To the men, she said, "Come over to the fire."

Her shapeless black dress was dry, but another just like it steamed on a screen near the hearth, along with a wide strip of piebald material. Her hair was twisted up into a turban made of another, similarly skewbald piece of cloth, tied in a lumpy knot over her brow. Thin frizzles of black-red hair fringed the turban's edge and hung to her shoulders. Her thick old skin looked all the whiter in contrast to that darkness; her eyes, the color of aquamarine, looked all the brighter.

"What takes you outside on such a day, Moder?" asked Kinnan, giving her the title out of courtesy.

"Stock still has to be fed and milked, and eggs still have to be gathered, rain or no rain, eh? They can't suddenly grow hands and do for themselves."

"He's... he's hurt," Brady managed to say, fumbling a gesture at Kinnan.

"So I see." To Kinnan, she said, "Sit at the table while I have a look at you. ...It's just a scratch. Soon mended." She told the hovering Brady to fetch a green pot of ointment from the shelf above the fireplace.

The mantle was lined with pots and fragrant packets. While he searched, he heard a light step behind him and heard the old woman say, "Put them on the table." He turned around to take the ointment to her, and nearly dropped it.

A slender figure stood over Kinnan, with one roughened hand still on the pile of cloth the old woman had demanded. Dull brown hair in braids, as men of that region often wore their hair, with russet highlights on the loose frizz, eyes brown and clear in a long face....

"Thanks, boy," Kinnan said.

"Boy?" said Brady. He dropped the medicine into Moder's outstretched hand on his way around the table. "Are you blind? It's Elsie!"

He threw his arms around the "boy," who froze in surprise. Brady drew back.

"Don't you know me, girl? Or are you pretending, to serve me out for what you think I did?" He looked from Elsie to the two at the table. "Kinnan's all right, if you're in disguise. He knows all about us. Landry's done a lot worse to him than he has to you, so you're safe with him. And you certainly don't think you're fooling *her*, do you?"

The old woman chuckled. "I know all about her, too, Young Master. But she doesn't, you see."

"I'm sorry," Elsie said. "You do seem to know me, but…. Who is 'Landry,' and what has he done to me? And – I *am* sorry – who are you, and how do we know each other? Are you my brother? …Are we sweethearts?"

"Mother forbid! Oh, by the Mother of Life, no!" Brady laughed. "If you were yourself, you'd never have said such a thing!"

"Do I dislike you?" Elsie smiled. "I can't imagine that."

"Well, bless my everlasting spirit," said Brady. "If I hadn't known you since you were knee-high to a sneer, I'd doubt you were you."

"She goes by the name of Edelin beren Cinnie," said the old woman, corking the ointment pot. "– Put this back, if you will, Young Master. – I found her on my beach, grumbling about being robbed."

Brady drew Elsie's purse from his sack and held it out to the girl. He felt ashamed, and potentially defiant: If she accepted his explanation, he was sorry for the trouble he'd caused her; if she wanted to be ugly about it, he was prepared to be ugly, too. "I meant to lift the coppers, to make sure I had enough for the food," he said, a sullen edge to his voice. "I got the silver, instead. Then I must have missed you in the woods. I didn't abandon you. I didn't rob you."

"I don't remember thinking so," said Elsie, vaguely. "I'm sorry if I misjudged you. I think, now, I should have known better." She took the money as if it were someone else's.

Brady looked to the old woman, hoping for some explanation of this wonder – this soft-spoken Elsie.

"I'm called Moder Zglaria," the old woman said, instead. "This is Wild Ass Island. You're welcome to stay, as long as you're willing to work."

"I'm Brady birn Ilka, from Kozabir." Brady turned his head toward Elsie but kept his eyes on Moder. "I'm not likely to forget that if I stay, am I?"

Moder chuckled again. "Maybe she needed to forget. Maybe she'll remember, when she needs to."

Elsie smiled, lifting her shoulders and palms-up hands. "This place is all I know. Come and dry off, and tell me about myself."

"Now that sounds like the Elsie I know," said Brady.

The men stripped as far as modesty would allow and draped their wet things on the firescreens. They rubbed themselves down with squares of flannel and dressed in dry clothes from their oilcloth packs.

Moder tucked her stray hair into her turban while Elsie served them all bowls of pot-luck from the kettle on the hearth, and mulled a jug of wine.

They ate, first. Then, as Moder lit a pipe and the three young people cleaned up after the meal, Elsie asked Brady again for her story. He told it – what he knew of it.

Moder drew on her pipe and pointed at Kinnan with the stem. "Now introduce yourself to the young lady, Kinnan-called-beren-Ada."

Brady felt a tingle, as if he had meant to sip water and tasted wine instead.

"How did you know?" Kinnan asked, a question Brady judged it foolish to ask this particular person.

Moder grunted and said, "Ten years is not that long ago, when you're as old as I am. Ten years ago, the true Kinninger disappeared – not far from here, as it happens – and a man named Kinnan claimed the throne, and a viper named Landry drove him into Kozabir. You come from Kozabir with a friend who calls you Kinnan, and you have a sword and a wound. It doesn't take an adept to piece you together, Young Master."

Kinnan touched the claw marks, already less painful under Moder's treatment. "I didn't get this fighting for my cause."

"It was a unicorn," Brady blurted.

Elsie drew a sharp breath. "A unicorn did that?"

"No, a mountain lion, after the unicorn. Its horn was stuck in a tree trunk – the unicorn's. Fighting the lion, I'd bet, and drove at it, and the lion leaped out of the way. I've heard of that happening."

"Farukh's tales," Kinnan scoffed.

"Well, we saw it, didn't we?"

Kinnan had nothing to say to that.

"I hit it with a rock or two – the lion – and it jumped at me. Kinnan fought it off, but–"

"My foot slipped," said Kinnan. "It got away. So did the thing we saw. Heart of the Way! What a beast the thing was! Not a unicorn, though. It couldn't have been. In all the old drawings, the thing is graceful, small and beautiful. This was...."

"He hit his head," said Brady, absently, gazing at the picture in his mind of the trapped, defiant beast. "I don't think he got a good clear look at it."

Moder waved the stem of her pipe at Brady, and spoke to Kinnan. "He's staying here until Edelin beren Cinnie remembers her past. Will we need to clear a spot for you, too, Kinnan beren Ada?"

"You... you believe in me? But why?"

"Let's just say *I* know the truth when I see it."

Brady had no doubt of that.

"I'm on my way to Pazni," Kinnan said. "I'm to meet a friend there."

"Pazni is nearly due east of here; there's a path just over the causeway."

"Then could I.... It might be safer if I could stay here and go into Pazni now and then to check."

"Or I could go," said Brady. "Except...." He stared at his hand, flexing it, turning it.

"Could I – or Brady – bring my friend back here?" Kinnan said.

Moder blew a puff or two, then nodded.

"But...," said Brady. He thought of his failed struggle to hold a chosen shape. Had he lost his ability? Even worse, had he lost control of it? He would be better off risking his true form in the first place, than coming back to it right in front of somebody.

"Let all worries go for now," said Moder. "We'll lay pallets for you two in here tonight. It's dark early with this rain. I don't fancy another wetting, turning out a stall in the twilight, do you? So let's call ourselves settled in."

Brady and Kinnan felt the loosening of knots they didn't realize were tied. They sat more comfortably on stool and floor and let their gazes be drawn into the fire in silence.

Moder broke into their reveries. "You, Brady – take that crock and come with me. We'll stir up some frumenty for tomorrow's breakfast. Edelin, you and the young beren Ada put down the pallets."

Brady followed the old woman down the steps to the cold room. Perhaps, he thought, he'd corner an answer down there.

"Cracked wheat," Moder said, measuring ingredients into the crock by handfuls and pinches. "Sugar. Raisins. Ground spice. Where's my dipper? Water. Always start with cold water, as cold as you can get."

"Who are you?" Brady asked bluntly.

"I'm Moder Zglaria. Are you always this forgetful, or do you need to escape a memory, too?"

"Nothing is what it seems here. I see shadows moving under the surface of everything here."

"Well, well, you're not a varier for nothing, are you?"

"...I didn't tell you I was a varier."

"Didn't you?"

"You know I didn't." Brady could feel his heart beating, steady, regular, but painfully hard. "...This place reeks of illusion."

Moder snorted. "Nonsense!"

"But I–"

"What you've said is nonsense. As pure as any nonsense can be, in this world."

"Why couldn't I hold my shape?"

"How should I know?"

"...This place is.........You're not...."

"Spit it out, boy, or swallow it."

"I can't say it right."

"You have to think it right, first." She started up the stairs, speaking to Brady over her shoulder. "These are stairs. This is a cold room. You're holding an earthenware pot. I'm an old woman. Everything here is truly what it seems to be." She pushed aside the curtain with her cane and waited for Brady to pass. As he did, she showed her blocky teeth and said, "At the very least."

"Kinnan's promised us a story," Elsie said, as Moder dropped the curtain. "About a unicorn."

"One of Farukh's," Kinnan said to Brady. "An old one, from Kozabir. You probably know it. About the poisoned well?"

Brady put the crock down where Moder pointed and said, in the tone of a man who doesn't intend to listen, "I know it."

~*~

Long, long ago (said Kinnan), when Matka Hayat – The Mother of Life – brought forth the world and everything in it, all the water in the world was drawn from one well. The First Animals shared the well in peace; drinking, washing, and watering their gardens like the good neighbors they were.

Seeing that everything was going along properly, the Matka ceased walking on the earth and became a part of it.

Then one day First Lion decided it didn't want to share.

"I'm the strongest and the fiercest," it boasted. "I should have all I want first, and dole out the rest to my friends."

Other animals disagreed, saying that all should be done as the Mother of Life had intended. The leader of these friends of the Mother was Unicorn. Its lieutenant was First Dog. Most warm-blooded animals, including First Bird, stood behind Unicorn and Dog. Even the snakes hissed at First Lion, and swore loyalty to the Mother. (Of course, no fish or eels took sides, because there were no water creatures at all at this time. This was before people, as well.)

First Cat said it wouldn't stand against its cousin, Lion, but it wouldn't stand against the Mother, either. It lay down with its head on its paws and its tail curled around its feet and pretended to close its eyes and watched.

First Lion said, "I have a present for anyone who will come over to me."

No one came except for two of the snakes: First Cobra and First Viper. Now at this time there was no venom in the world. But when Cobra and Viper joined First Lion, Lion spat in each of their mouths, and they became poisonous. Each one had also bitten the ends off the tails of First Lizard, First Frog, and First Toad. In fact, Cobra bit off all of Frog's tail, and it's never grown back. First Lion turned these tail-tips into whole lizards and frogs and toads. This is why some lizards, some toads, and some frogs are poisonous, while most are not.

Now First Lion took First Cobra and put it down the well. It stayed there all day and threatened to bite animals who tried to draw water unless they promised to serve Lion. In the evening, Cobra came out and Viper held the well all night.

~*~

"In the well?" said Elsie, wide-eyed and blinking. "A serpent? How big? What color?"

"The story doesn't say. Do you know, Brady?"

"No, I don't." Brady began to take an interest, not so much in the story as in Elsie's reaction to it.

"Do you know, Moder?" asked Kinnan.

"I always heard it was a hundred feet long, big around as a man's thumb, and dull green with a white belly."

"Oh...," said Elsie.

"That was the cobra," said Moder. "And I always heard the viper was the same size, but striped red and yellow."

"Oh," said Elsie, again. "I'm sorry, Kinnan. Go on."

Some of the First Insects said they would try to talk other animals into serving. They were given water and venom and began crawling and buzzing and biting the other animals, tormenting them and spreading diseases.

The sick, thirsty animals lay down in despair. When they woke, they were no longer First Animals, for each had split into two: male and female. Two of a kind cuts trouble in half, and the first offspring of a couple is Hope.

When First Lion saw Matka's animals in pairs, it was jealous. It bit its servants in half; where their blood spilled are the deserts. Each half became male or female. Lion cut itself to pieces with its claws, and became males and females of all the different sorts of lion in the world.

So all the creatures began to multiply and shrink to the forms they have today except Unicorn. It remained singular and unique, but it grew in size and power until, one day, it led a rush on the well. It speared the cobra inside the well and tossed him over its shoulder.

The Mother's creatures drank and washed and watered their gardens as before. They even shared with First Lion's creatures.

That was nearly their undoing, for the mate of the dead cobra pretended to be dying of thirst. She hung over the rim of the well for a long time, but she wasn't drinking – She was emptying herself of all her venom and all her poisoned blood. She spread out the skin just behind her head to hide what she was doing, and cobras have had that ability ever since.

When one of the Mother's animals touched the cobra's mate to ask her to let someone else have a turn, her empty skin whirled away to become the first deadly wind storm.

The water in the well was undrinkable, except for the lions and poisonous beasts.

Matka's animals went to Unicorn and begged it to lead them again to some sort of victory.

"We will die," they said, "and all our young will die, and Matka's earth will be left to our killers."

"Then let it be so," said Unicorn. "Matka brought forth the lions and the venomous animals just as she brought us forth. It might be that the earth was meant for them all along, and we were meant for death. Dead or alive, we're Matka's creatures, aren't we?"

Then the animals were angry. All of them except the dogs and cats and birds plotted against the Unicorn. They made a net of vines and caught Unicorn in it, tangling its horn in the web and tying it so that it couldn't move its head. They threw stones at it until it was bloody and broken."

~*~

"Oh, no!" said Elsie.

"It's just a story," Brady said.

"I don't want to hear any more, if they kill it."

"What's the difference?" asked Moder Zglaria. "It said Life or Death was no matter. Besides, as Young Master Varier says, it's only a story."

"But it's so awful, if—"

"No, no, Matka Hayat saves it," Kinnan reassured the girl. "I might as well finish."

"All right," Elsie said, warily.

~*~

Meanwhile, the cats continued to sit apart, not helping the Unicorn or its attackers. The dogs and birds lifted their voices, begging Matka Hayat to come and save her servant.

Matka Hayat sprang from the earth. All the animals bowed down before her in terror, because they knew they had done a wicked thing.

"Unicorn delivered the well to you once," she said, "and now, when he offers you wisdom instead of mere water, you repay him with hatred and harm. For that, you will be less than you are now. You will be less than these stones that struck my most faithful servant by your hand."

She made all the animals to be just as they are today, with each one's paw and claw and beak raised against the others, and little understanding between them. But to the birds she gave the gift of song, because they had called her on Unicorn's behalf. To the dogs she gave the howls and barks they use to mourn and sound alarms.

Then Matka passed the shadow of her hand over the stones and they became people. Matka gave the animals to them. She told the people to take the bloodied vines off Unicorn and throw them into the well. Immediately, the water turned pure and good.

Matka snapped her fingers. The well's rim crumbled and the water overflowed, spreading over the world in streams and rivers and seas. The vines broke apart and became fish and eels and other water creatures.

Matka healed Unicorn's hurts. Then she said to it, "You alone are left of my First Creatures. Will you come with me out of Mortal Life, or will you stay in it alone?"

"It is all one to me," said Unicorn.

"Then let it be so," said Matka, and she became part of the earth again, leaving Unicorn to haunt the world in her name.

None of the animals remember anything that happened at the beginning of the world, and the humans weren't there.

But – When the place where Unicorn suffered was deserted, a cat crept up and sniffed it. She found a fleck of blood and licked it up, and cats remember it all.

This story was told to me by an old woman, who said she had it from her grandmother, and her grandmother had it from her grandmother, and her grandmother had it – from her cat.

~*~

Elsie applauded, her face shining. "What a wonderful story!"

"And it proves what we saw," said Brady. "It looked like something you could throw stones at for quite a while without doing it much major damage. And Kinnan – show them what you found."

Kinnan unbuttoned his pocket and drew out the striped shreds, holding them reverently on his palm. "Alicorn."

Elsie stretched out a trembling finger. At Kinnan's nod, she touched them. A shudder ran through her.

"I can almost see it," she whispered. "Bigger than a horse, much bigger. Its horn, as long as my arm. You can feel its heart beating. You can feel it breathing. There's a sweetness... deeper than a smell...."

"You've seen it, too," said Brady.

"Did you feel all that?" Elsie asked.

"No, but.... How many legs did yours have?"

"...I don't remember. If I really saw it at all, I didn't see it clearly. Maybe that's why I felt so much."

"It had four legs, of course," said Kinnan. "How many legs should it have?"

"Three," said Brady. "Like the one we saw."

"It didn't have–"

"How would you know?" said Brady, more violently than he had intended. "You thought it was a horse!"

"Three legs," said Moder. "That's right, isn't it?"

"Where does that come in the story?" Kinnan asked. "I never heard that part."

"It isn't in the story," said Brady. "It isn't in any story. That's just the way it is. Everybody knows that."

Kinnan laughed. "Everybody in Kozabir, maybe; but, in Layounna, unicorns have four legs."

"Like regular horses," said Brady. "And they're little, and pretty, and prance around with flowers in their manes and tails."

Moder quaked with silent laughter, tears popping out of the corners of her eyes.

"What's funny?" Kinnan asked.

"You," said Moder. "Sitting there, displaying relics as evidence of something you don't even seem to believe in."

Kinnan closed his thumb over the curls and quirked one side of his mouth in a cynical smile. "Lightning can do peculiar things to wood. If one form of damage goes by the name of 'alicorn' and people believe it comes from a mythical beast, the power I get from it is real. Let me show you something else." He reached into his pack. "This is what will finally win me the throne, and keep it for me, too."

He pulled out a bundle, untied it, unwrapped it, and lifted a bag. It was made of cloth of gold, with small tiles of silver sewn to it.

"Quite a tobacco pouch," said Brady.

Kinnan didn't bother with a squelching look. "It's a mandate bag."

"Yours?" said Moder.

"Of course, mine. I told you who I am. You said you believed me. Whose else would it be?"

"I only asked."

Kinnan put the alicorn into the pouch. "Some of the old people say the true royal line – my line – the House of Onagros – held the throne by right of mandate, represented by a bag. None of the old folk agreed on what was in it except for one item – alicorn. Now I have that. The other things…
Some say amber. Some say silver. Some say dried clay made from ashes, fertile soil, and the blood of a white dove."

"Ugh!" Moder screwed up her face and pushed Kinnan's words away with hand and pipe. "Blood of a white dove…. Prick your finger and use the blood of an ass, instead."

Kinnan laughed, shrugged, and put the bag away.

Brady lay awake that night, his mind a confusion of vivid impressions that were almost thoughts. When at last the rain on the cottage thatch lulled him to sleep, he dreamed.

He saw Kinnan go up to one of those sugary "Layounnan unicorns." When Kinnan touched it, it proved to be made of paper, and he folded it up and put it in his mandate bag. Kinnan disappeared and Elsie rode up on the "Kozabirian unicorn," its three feet sinking into the earth with every step but leaving no impression behind, not even a bent blade of grass. Then the girl wasn't Elsie, but the woman in Kozabirian dress who smiled her way through so many of Brady's dreams. She wasn't smiling now, though, she was crying. Her tears, falling to the ground from the back of the unicorn, sounded like rain on thatch. She held out a hand to him. The silvery earring Salali had given him tingled, and he heard the girl's voice: "There you are! Come here! Come here! Oh, help me! I don't know what to do!"

"I know!" said Brady, and woke.

He raised himself on one elbow and looked guiltily at the others, afraid he'd disturbed them.

All three were still; all three breathed deeply and evenly.

Brady felt something he recognized, but couldn't immediately identify. It was a closeness among the four that was like being connected by bonds of some fluid power. It was like a unison in the face of something other. An odd feeling to have in this company, and one Kinnan would be glad to claim the benefit of. And maybe that was right. Maybe helping oust the House of Sarpa was a way to repay the Layounnan woman who had died saving his younger self.

For that's what this feeling was like – It was like a boy and his family, powerless against a snake, their several beings focused into one, as if they could defeat the threat by the strength of their unified rejection of it.

chapter 11
cat of the inland sea

The day Nerissa began keeping "house" for Tartarus, he woke her soon after dawn with a nudge of his grubby foot. The lean-to door was open and Nerissa could see the painful glinting of the sea, though the shed was still in shadow.

Tartarus loomed above her, bare from the waist up, tall, thick, hook-nosed. "You look like a fright in the morning, young runaway. Ever hear of a comb?"

"I could ask you the same." She glared at the stringy black tangles streaming from his head and face like dirty water.

"Pert talk for a little girl."

"I told you last night – I'm ten. Maybe eleven."

"Look more like eight. Of course, you look like a plucked chicken, yet you claim to be human, so can I trust your claims?"

Nerissa thrust herself out of the tattered blankets Tartarus had thrown to her the night before, pointedly ignoring him.

Tartarus went back to his own nest of rags and rummaged in them. He fished out a sleeveless shirt and drew it on and left it unbuttoned. He scratched at whatever of his grayish-brown skin he could reach.

"Start the day with a little fruit." His guttural voice sounded immensely smug, as if he had invented this precept. He dug a small, hard, wrinkled apple out of a dirty canvas bag and tossed it to Nerissa.

She bit into it. It was dry and sour, with only a faint hint of sweetness. She ate it, though.

"Tasty?" Tartarus asked.

"No. Hungry."

"Toss the core in the fireplace," he said, although he had eaten his apple stem and all. Nerissa had choked a bit at seeing him, afraid he would expect her to do the same.

She had been too tired last night to register much, but this morning – perhaps because of a draft pulled down the chimney and out the open door – she was aware of a familiar scent. Now she recognized it as the smell of old food and rubbish rotting in a mixed pile. The fireplace would be the first thing she cleaned – if she didn't run away.

"I'm going out to fish, girl. Keep a sharp ear and a sharp eye, and if you see or hear anyone coming – *anyone* – close and latch the door and don't open it on any persuasion. Might be a slaver or a slaver's informer. Understand?"

"Yes."

"An informer might be anyone, even somebody you think you know. Somebody you think is a friend. Understand?"

"Yes, I understand."

"Sometimes slavers even use an animal to hunt out escaped slaves. Like a bird."

"A bird?"

"I've seen men use birds to fish for them, to hunt other birds for them, even hunt rabbits for them. Why not people? You can't be too careful."

All the same, Nerissa knew she trusted her bird more than she trusted Tartarus by an immeasurably wide margin.

"I'll be back tonight with fish for supper. If you get hungry during the day, there's some berry bushes up above. If you don't fall and break your neck getting to them, the bluish black ones are the best."

"I understand," Nerissa said, before Tartarus could ask.

"There's a freshwater pool up there, too, if you get thirsty. Keep a lookout, though."

"I will."

Tartarus turned in the doorway as he left and held up an admonitory finger, but said no more.

Now: Stay or go? Tartarus claimed she owed him a day's work, but he also said he wouldn't be back till night, and she could be far away by then. She doubted he'd come after her. Still, she couldn't quite dismiss the cold shine of his eyes when he cautioned her not to lie – to him. She had a feeling he wouldn't find much humor in her stealing anything from him, even something as valueless as a day of her life.

Nerissa began her work by keeping her promise to herself. That nasty fireplace.... How did Tartarus cook the fish he caught? He probably ate his fish raw – bones, head, tail, scales, and fins.

Shuddering at that thought, she raked the refuse onto one of Tartarus' bedcloths, then carried it out and dumped it where a patch of dirt had settled in a depression of the rock. If she stayed, she thought she might start a little garden like the ones in Granitz. Radishes and greens. Onions.

She used Tartarus' same bedcloth to dust off the broom and shelves. She took all the rags outside and shook them, then spread them on the rocks with some vague notion of letting the sun cook them clean.

It wasn't yet noon, but she was hungry. She climbed – carefully – around the overhang to the top of the bluff. There, spread before her, was moorland covered with a carpet of flowers in every shade of purple from indigo to blushing white. Rocks, boulders, and crags erupted from the uneven ground, but plowed fields were visible beyond, visible for a long way. She couldn't have walked that far... yet there was no sign of Granitz, no sign of anything she remembered passing. She hadn't walked over that rocky land, hadn't passed furrowed earth. Yet she must have, if she had come from where she had started to where she was now.

She turned and looked down at the coastline. Ribbons of seaweed drying on the shore told even a town-dweller like Nerissa that the tide was out. She saw sand, spits of higher ground, the odd boulder, but nowhere – nowhere within her wide range of vision – was there a jumble of rocks leading into the sea.

But there was such beauty.... Nerissa forgot the puzzle in the glory of it.

There were some bushes nearby, heavy with blue and blue-black berries – these must be the ones Tartarus had been talking about. Nerissa picked a berry and tasted it; it was sweet. She gathered a handful of berries, sat down among the leathery leaves, and ate.

When Tartarus returned at sunset, the lean-to was swept and dusted, the bedcloths aired and folded. The worst of the dents had been beaten out of the old pots and pans. Nerissa had gathered dead brush from the moor and laid a fire. A bowl of the blue-black berries stood on the hearth, there being no table.

"Well, aren't we nice?" said Tartarus. "Aren't we sweet and clean and home-like?"

"You said I owed it to you," Nerissa snapped. She braced herself for the blow that Barand had always paid for such "backtalk," and flinched from the shock when no blow came.

"Do you know how to clean fish, girl?"

Nerissa shook her head.

Tartarus grunted. "Thought not. I cleaned 'em myself. Now I'll show you how to cook them. Know how to start a fire?"

"We always got a pan of hot ashes from a neighbor whenever we had anything to burn."

"Show you how to use a tinderbox." Tartarus held out his broad, flat hand and laughed aloud as Nerissa drew back. The black wooden box, as big as Nerissa's palm but less than half the size of the man's, was in the shape of a tortoise with his head and legs drawn in. "Thought you weren't scared of Tortoise."

With a defiant glare, Nerissa slapped the box.

Tartarus laughed again. He squatted before the pile of dry bushes in the fireplace. Nerissa watched him crush some twigs to tinder, then take out the flint and steel and strike a spark, then another, then another. The tinder caught, and soon the larger pieces were flaming.

"Give me that flat pan while this burns down." Tartarus reached into the burlap pocket tied at his waist and drew out four fish fillets still streaked with blood and speckled with whatever had been in his pocket before. "I suppose you want to wash these."

"I'm not particular," said Nerissa, trying to sound disinterested, "but the fish might be."

"I'm not climbing back down, just to fetch water."

"Down?"

"To the Sea, girl. Sea water's got more flavor than that vapid stuff up there." He shoved a thumb, colored with the insides of fish, toward the freshwater pool above. "Bland as the milk of the Mother of Life."

This impiety shocked even Nerissa, who knew little and cared less for religion.

"I'll get the water," was all she said.

She took a pot and clambered down to the shore, waded out a little into the water and filled the pot nearly full. She slopped some out, carrying it back up the slope, but the pot was still more than half full when she put it down in the shack.

Tartarus sloshed the fish in the water and tossed three of the fillets into the pan. "You can't eat more than one tonight. We'll leave the other one in the pot and stew it for breakfast."

Pocket fluff and all, thought Nerissa.

"Never would have expected a guttersnipe like you to be so delicate in her tastes," said Tartarus, as if he had heard.

The girl had never been accused of an excess of refinement before. The thought made her smile, even as the intended insult sparked her temper.

"That's a savage look," Tartarus observed, a note of approval in his voice.

The brush had settled down to lumps of glowing charcoal. Tartarus raked the lumps into a circle and set a high trivet over it. He put the pan of fillets on the trivet and sat back. The oily fish soon began to sizzle and filled the shack with a rich smell. Nerissa's stomach rumbled. She reached for a berry but Tartarus scooped up a handful first, scrabbling in the bowl with his gummy fingers.

"It isn't me," Nerissa said, no longer hungry for those berries. "It's you."

"What are you talking about, girl?"

"It isn't me that's delicate. It's you – you're disgusting."

"I am, am I? Maybe you'd like to spend the night on the beach."

"I wouldn't do that. I'd go up. I'd spend the night up there."

"Cold. Wild animals." Tartarus leaned toward her with narrowed eyes and hissed, "Tortoise'll get you."

"Tortoise had better look out for me. I saw tortoises for sale in the marketplace in Granitz. They make soup out of tortoises, and medicine out of their shells –" An acrid odor made Nerissa's nose prickle. "The fish! They're burning!"

"I think you're right!" Tartarus reached past Nerissa to grab one of her bedcloths and used it to pull the skillet off the trivet and onto the stone floor. "Get down one of those plates." He up-ended the pan and shook it; the three fillets plopped out, black on one side and barely done on the other.

"That's disgusting!" said Nerissa. "You did that on purpose!"

"If you don't like the way I cook, do it yourself."

"I wish I had!"

"As of now, the job's yours!"

"…As of now?"

"From now on, starting with breakfast tomorrow. I get my own lunch, but starting tomorrow you clean the fish and you cook the fish."

"From now on…," said Nerissa softly. That sounded permanent. That made her sound like a person with a place in the world. Impulsively, she laid a small hand on Tartarus' leathery arm.

"Get off me!" he growled. "Get away! I'm trying to eat my supper."

Nerissa pulled her hand back.

Tartarus held up that warning finger Nerissa was coming to know. "Never do that again. I live alone because I don't like people clutching at me. I don't like you and I don't want your affection. Is that clear?"

"Yes."

She used her fingers as Tartarus did to snap off sections of blackened fish, and scooped the cooked side off with her teeth.

"Good, eh?" said Tartarus with a grin, as Nerissa grimaced at the bitter taste.

"Almost as good as the apple this morning."

For the next few minutes, there was no sound but the crunch of teeth on burnt fish. Then, from outside, came the song of a bird, a song Nerissa knew.

Tartarus moved more quickly than Nerissa would have thought he could, rising and closing the door, blocking out the last rays of sun and dropping the latch with a firm *thunk*.

In the sudden near-darkness, Nerissa groped for a thick chunk of brush and shoved it into the coals. The twigs caught and flared up, showing Tartarus wiping his mouth on his arm, then his hands on his short trousers. He came back to the hearth, stooping toward the bowl of berries. Nerissa, affecting not to see him, picked up the bowl and emptied it into the pot with the water and the last fish fillet. As the bark burned off the brush and the flames died down to a smoldering glow, she put the pot on the trivet to stew until morning.

"Nicely done, girl," said Tartarus. "I see you don't like me, either."

Nerissa didn't answer.

~*~

In the morning, Nerissa sat up and started moving as soon as Tartarus opened the door. Before he had finished scratching himself, she had taken down two bowls, two stained wooden spoons, and a ladle. Carefully, she dished out fish and berries for herself, inspecting each scoop before she accepted it. The rest, she poured out for Tartarus.

"I think I like having a servant," Tartarus said.

I hope you like eating what you grubbed out of your pocket yesterday, because that's what you're eating.

"Don't get up to any mischief while I'm gone today," Tartarus said as he left. "Stay close. Don't talk to anybody or anything. Do as you're told and maybe I'll teach you something."

"How to clean fish?"

With a toothy grin Nerissa could only suppose was meant to be enticing, Tartarus leaned over with his hands on his knees and said, "How would you like to be invisible, girl? Go anywhere, do anything, and never be caught. Theft, revenge.... You could live in the Emir's palace, and nobody would know. Never be afraid of anything ever again."

I'm not afraid now. The realization surprised her.

"Think about it. I can teach you. You may not think it to look at me but I know things, girl. I know things."

When he had gone, Nerissa did think about it. She thought about it as she carried the dirty dishes down to the beach and scoured the skillet with sand. She was still thinking about it when a loud *miaouw* interrupted her.

A cat leapt onto a dune just out of her reach. It sat amid the clumps of tough grass, staring at her through half-closed eyes.

Nerissa had never seen a cat like it before. It was a mixture of black and red-orange, with pale orange eyes, and it was bigger than the cats of Granitz. Although it was thin, it wasn't half-starved, which was also different from the cats Nerissa had known. Its coat was dull and staring, as if it had never learned to groom itself.

It gave another *miaouw*, a deep and demanding sound, and Nerissa at once began thinking of the cat as "He."

"Are you hungry?" she asked. "Hungry, little man?" She scraped the scant leavings out of her bowl and the stew pot into Tartarus' bowl and set it at arm's length. Then she turned a little away from the cat and went on with her work, watching out of the corner of her eye.

Her experience with the cats of Granitz led her to expect the cat would creep up to the food and eat if she pretended disinterest. This cat yawned, stretched, and walked up to the bowl as if he had never had to dodge for safety.

Nerissa wondered if the cat belonged to somebody or if, on the contrary, he had had too little dealing with people to know he should be careful of them. She stopped working and turned back toward the animal. He went on eating. She reached out and touched the tip of his ear. He put his ears back and hissed off-handedly, but didn't move away.

When the cat had finished, Nerissa scoured his bowl and washed the sand out in the sea.

"Goodbye, cat," she said, as she started back up the slope to Tartarus' shack.

When she had put her load away, though, she found the cat had followed her.

"You'd better not stay." She regretted having fed him; Tartarus, she felt sure, would disapprove of an animal around the place. He might drive the cat away. He might kill him. "Shoo!"

She made a half-hearted flap or two in the cat's direction, and couldn't tell whether she was glad or sorry when he ignored her and curled up just outside the door, where the sun was beginning to warm the rocky ledge.

Nerissa came back out and sat beside the cat. He got up, moved two inches away, and lay down again.

The girl sighed. "Won't you let me pet you?" She pulled her knees up and wrapped her arms around them, her cheek on her kneecaps. This was the only embrace she had ever known and, as always, it was less than satisfying.

"I'm glad I ran away," she told the cat. "But I wish.... I thought my bird was leading me to someplace better." She raised her head and looked out to sea. "Well, this is better than home. Tartarus doesn't beat me. I think he's going to let me stay. I believe he's going to let me sleep indoors every night, even if he does tease about it. He acts like he cares whether I eat or not. That's better." She sighed again and returned her gaze to the cat, who had his head turned away from her. "I just wish.... Everybody belongs somewhere. I don't. Do you think Tartarus will let me belong here, if I stay long enough and don't make him too mad? He doesn't seem to mind getting mad, though."

Slowly, as if she knew better but couldn't help herself and didn't really want to, Nerissa reached out and stroked the cat's back.

He turned in a flash and caught her hand between his jaws, his eyes slitted, a high-pitched snarl coming from the back of his throat.

Nerissa jumped, but held her hand still, meeting that narrow glare with a calm regard, one wild animal at another's mercy.

The cat bit down just hard enough to nip the skin, then released the child's hand and leapt up, back arched, tail bushed, screaming with what sounded like rage. He bounded away and was gone.

Nerissa inspected the pin-pricks on her hand and smiled. "You didn't bite me. You wanted to, but you wanted *not* to, more."

~*~

She waited for Tartarus on the beach, too happy to stay close to the shack. That earned her a frown, when Tartarus paddled around a high point of land and into sight.

"Told you to stay close – to watch out."

"I've been watching," she told him, not saying that she'd been watching, in vain, for the cat's return.

When Tartarus landed, he pulled a thick string which hung off the stern of the boat and raised a net bag. It flapped with the struggles of a pair of fish.

Not much of a fisherman, if it takes him all day to collect no more than that. Then she reasoned that he probably caught much more, but sold them somewhere before returning home with just enough for supper.

"Hold that." He gave the bag to Nerissa. "By the string, girl, like this – those fins can cut! Carry them over to that rock. You can put them down, but keep hold of the string or they'll flop all over the beach."

He stowed his boat and came back. Drawing a knife Nerissa hadn't known he wore, he squatted by the rock and clubbed each fish in the head with the handle. Then he put the knife on the rock, took Nerissa by the shoulders, and shook her.

"I say stay close, I mean stay close. Didn't I tell you?"

"Y-yes."

"Who's been here today? Who have you seen? Who have you spoken to?"

"Nobody."

"And no thing?"

After an internal tug-of-war, Nerissa said, "A cat. He didn't stay long."

"Feed him?"

Nerissa nodded.

"Tried to pet him too. I'd bet on it."

Nerissa held out her bitten hand.

"Serves you right. You won't try it again."

"Yes I will. It's none of your business, anyway; you don't care if he takes my hand off up to the elbow, so don't pretend you do."

"You'll get cat-scratch fever, and then what am I supposed to do with you?"

"Put me out Up There," said Nerissa, meaning on the moor. "Let me die. It's nothing to you, and I don't care."

There was a silent moment, in which the two traded unamiable stares, then Tartarus picked up his knife.

"Here's how you clean fish, girl. Pay attention."

~*~

The cat didn't come the next day, though Nerissa saved some of her morning stew for him. She spent the day on the moor, peeking over the ledge now and then, hoping for a glimpse of black and red-orange. She listened for the song of her bird, but neither came.

When Tartarus rowed ashore that evening, he shoved the bag of fish and a knife into Nerissa's hands and said, "You know how to do this now. I'm going to have a nap." He stopped after a few steps, turned, and said, "Any more cats today? Or anything?"

Nerissa shook her head. "I was alone." She tried to sound indifferent, but she heard the sadness and resentment in her voice. She hoped Tartarus didn't hear it. She doubted she'd get much comfort from him if he did.

"Alone's the best way to be," he said. "Easier."

When Nerissa didn't answer or argue, he walked on.

Nerissa waited, watching him climb to the shelf and enter the lean-to. She cocked her head to catch any sound. A rain of heather and other blooms flew from the shack and fell pattering to the sand.

Tartarus loomed in the doorway, scowling down at her. "Posies!" he boomed.

Nerissa laughed so hard she had to sit down.

"Bah!" said Tartarus, and disappeared into the hovel.

~*~

She was nearly finished cleaning the fish when the cat leapt, seemingly from nowhere, onto the offal and began to eat.

"There you are. Where have you been?" The animal didn't look up at the sound of her voice. "Cat, I'll tell you what: We like each other, he and I. We do."

The cat growled, sorting through the debris with the tip of a claw.

"Oh, not much, but a little. Maybe enough that I belong to him, even if we do fight. I used to know a lot of people who fought, but they belonged to each other." Nerissa cut a piece of flesh from one of the fillets she had just cleaned and put it before the cat. "That's nicer than guts, isn't it?" She rubbed the top of the cat's skull with the knob on the knife's handle.

The cat ducked and flattened his ears, but when she began again he didn't move or growl, not even when she changed the knife for her fingertips. When she tried to stroke the scruffy back, the cat slid away.

~*~

"Thought any more about my offer, girl?" Tartarus asked over that night's fish. "Want to learn? Be invisible? It'll take a while – it doesn't come easy. It doesn't come cheap, either."

"I can't pay. You know I can't pay."

"Well, housekeeping, to begin with. And I'll show you how to gather shells." He held his thumb and forefinger close together, to measure the size he meant. "The village women make jewelry out of 'em for the inland ladies to wear. Then, after a lesson or two, you can start stealing."

Nerissa frowned. "I don't like stealing."

"Oh," said Tartarus, "forgive me. I forgot you were so fine. Never stole so much as a penny in your life, have you?"

"I didn't say I never did it. I said I don't like it. It's mean."

"Steal from the rich – they can afford it. Steal from the poor – they can't do anything about it." He slapped his bare thigh and laughed.

Nerissa turned her back on him.

After a time of silence, Tartarus said, "Well, do you want to learn or don't you?"

Nerissa shook her head. "I've been next to invisible all my life. I don't want to make it worse."

"Here, girl, you're not crying, are you? I won't have a sniveler in the place. Get out, if you're going to cloud up and rain."

Nerissa left the shack and climbed to the moor. She half hoped Tartarus would come after her, but she knew he wouldn't.

She went to sleep in the dew-drenched heather, but woke up the next morning in her place against the wall, wrapped in her bedcloths.

Neither she nor Tartarus said anything about it.

CHAPTER 12
WAYFARER'S DOG

Elsie milked the goats and Kinnan split wood into kindling. The scratches on his scalp seemed to have disappeared overnight, with only a lingering tenderness in the area marking where the cougar's paw had struck.

Brady, barefoot, sleeves tied back and trews rolled up to above his knees, scrubbed at the stone floor with a bundle of woven twigs and vinegar-water.

"Phew, what a smell!" he said, as he started. By the time he was half-way down the room, his mind turned to boiled greens, and he found the vinegar sparking his appetite.

Moder sat on her bed, spinning a fine thread out of flax.

Brady worked in silence for a while, enjoying the homely sound Moder's drop spindle made when it clicked against the floor. Little by little, the spinning seemed to gain importance, until he felt the same awe of the old woman he'd felt when he first saw her.

When Brady reached Moder's feet, he stopped work and looked up at her. "Moder...."

The old woman cocked her eyes at him and grunted, to show she was listening.

"Don't riddle me, or mock me, or tell me you don't know what I'm talking about. I need your help."

After a moment, Moder said, "Well, then?"

"I... dream about a woman. One certain woman. No one I've ever met. Salali – an old trinket-maker – gave me this...." He fingered the love-knot in his ear. "She said.... I'm not quite sure if she ever said what it would do, but she said I'd find my sweetheart."

"Don't you believe her?"

"I think," Brady said, miserably, "she might have been humoring me.

Comforting words from a wise old woman to a callow youth – that kind of thing."

"And what do you want from me, boy? More of the same?"

"More. Something… more."

Moder shifted, gathering herself to rise, and Brady knotted his hand in her skirt, as if he could hold her in place.

"Take me to serve you. Not as an apprentice; take me as a common servant. Let it be for as long or short as you like. Help me find that girl – or help me stop dreaming about her. Please."

When Moder said nothing, he went on. "I'm a varier. A Kozabirian and a dabbler in the Things Beyond. A very small-time dabbler, and that's all I want to be, but it's given me… it's given me an awareness and a hunger, and you're the answer to both."

Moder put one of her broad, white hands on the hand Brady had twisted in her skirt. "I know that awareness of something out of place. And that hunger for the proper… union… of one… thing…." As the old woman spoke, her words seemed to come with more difficulty, as if these words were tufts of grass, roots entwined with so many other roots they couldn't be pulled up cleanly.

She shook her head with an irritated snort. "Listen to this, then. – In patience. When the House of Onagros held the throne of Layounna, it ruled imperfectly, but it ruled well. Then the old, old Kinninger, father of the mother of the one Landry wed and murdered, lost the balance between power and burden. He lost the connection between self-indulgence and generosity. Each generation after him let pleasure outweigh prudence. Still, they weren't far from the heart of harmony; it's part of their heritage, part of their blood. One of that line, before long, would have regained the path. But, now…."

Moder gave Brady's hand a gentle squeeze. "Do you think this is just Wayfaring prattle?"

"I know the difference between a fair land and a pressed one."

"But you wonder what it has to do with me. Or you."

"No. I don't wonder. It doesn't matter. I'm caught in something. I have been, since I saw your light last night, maybe since long before that. I'm not one to close my eyes and let events carry me along, but I know better than to swim upstream. I've landed at your feet, Moder Zglaria of Fiddlewood. What now?"

He waited, while Moder gazed, unseeing, at the oiled hide covering the window.

"Sorcha beren Ada," she said at last, "Kinnan's half-sister, and heir before him to Layounna's throne, is cloistered at Kudasad Waystation. If it pleases you to serve me, serve her."

"…Why? Why that?"

"There's an animal in Kudasad called a meerkat, I believe. I understand they kill serpents."

Brady grinned, thinking of the long, thin animals, not much bigger than the sand squirrels with whom they sometimes shared their burrows. "Cobras," he said. "They kill cobras."

"If they see a cobra at a distance, they don't avoid it, but go and provoke it into fighting, don't they?"

Brady nodded, then laughed. "If I'm a meerkat, who could be the snake? Not His Grace, Landry Oliva beren Ada, by any chance?" The varier pulled a face, as if he were trying to make himself into a caricature of Landry, forgetting his loss of ability. "I've provoked that particular cobra once and lived to tell about it. He's an enemy of my mistress, Devona's. If serving Sorcha beren Ada equals a biff on the head to Landry, I'd do it for fun, if nothing else."

"This is deadly earnest, boy. Death holds no terrors for me, but does it hold none for you? Don't you understand that the head of one thing must swallow the tail of another to complete a circle?"

"Don't you understand that I don't have a choice?"

"I tell you, boy, you are free to choose. You are free. I tell you so."

"The more you free me, the more I'm bound."

"I bind you, then, if that frees you."

Brady's eyes and Moder's held; his, opaque and black, hers, blue-green and clear as living water.

"I'll know when I'm free," he said.

"I know. It's a heavy burden, liberty to choose our own shackles. Go to Sorcha, then, at Kudasad Waystation."

"And how do I serve her, once I find her?"

Moder Zglaria shrugged. "How would I know? Ask her."

"And my dreams? The woman? Is Sorcha beren Ada the woman in my dreams? Is that what you mean?"

"Have a look at her, and see what you think." She touched Brady's silvery love-knot. "The woman who made this knows her business – more deeply than she understands, may be."

"Really?" Brady caressed the ear-baub, feeling the warmth left in it by the old woman's brief touch. "I will find her, then?"

"Your sweetheart?" Moder showed her blocky teeth and held back a chuckle. "You'll find her."

So he finished his work and slipped away, trusting Moder Zglaria with goodbyes and explanations to the others. He had no sooner left the cottage than he felt a tingle. He had no sooner left the island than he felt a surge, like the foaming of beer when it's tapped from a dusty keg into a clear glass. He sprang into the air, spread hawk wings, and flew south.

When he landed in the outskirts of Kudasad, he was surprised at the intensity of his longing for a visit with Elsie's mother. But it was evening, and there would be no Devona without Darcy, and Darcy was easy to resist. Besides, there would be time for visits when the quest was over.

Brady made himself into a large black dog and loped to the Waystation.

He prowled and sniffed and listened. Someone called, "Sorcha," and a woman's voice answered from the garden. A window closed. He rounded a corner with the woman from his dreams as clear in his mind as a painted portrait.

This woman was not the end of that search. She was the end of an older one. Her features, the way the weary lines of her face turned to compassion in her eyes, even the silver strands in her red-brown hair – They were all impressed on him as deeply as the lookfeel of his own mother.

And now he knew who had given her life to save him – him, a stranger's boy and a foreigner. How could he have guessed? Who would ever have guessed? Kinninger Karol beren Ada, in flight from the rebellion of her consort and the murder of her heart-husband, the sister of Kinnan beren Ada, whose urge for revenge he had mocked, true Kinninger of this country, whose throne and succession he had held so lightly and spoken of so blithely…she, Karol beren Ada, had died obscurely in saving a random child.

He thought again of the play his real-life story echoed, of the crown on the brow of the dragon, and wondered again at the parallel.

The knowledge gave Brady no sense of Destiny or Greater Purpose: the Kinninger's death magnified *her*, not him. In gratitude, in shame, in humility, in the tribute of his heart and of his dead parents' hearts as well, he lay down as a dog at Sorcha's feet.

He would have gone into the Stationhouse with Sorcha, but her quiet, "No," stopped him on the threshold. He lay down and waited, and was still there when she came outside again.

He showed no interest in the other cloistered women or in Mistress Brina, but waited for Sorcha and followed where she would let him follow.

By his second day, he was accepted as an unofficial pet. By the third, he was acknowledged as Sorcha's. Scraps and bones put by for him were given to her first. As Sorcha grew more attached to the animal, she felt less foolish about testing those scraps against the alicorn pendant Mistress Brina had given her.

Brady waited, his patience thinning but holding, for the form of his service to clarify.

One night, it rained – a thundering deluge like the one through which he'd seen the unicorn.

The Stationhouse door opened and Sorcha whistled him in.

"Mistress Brina makes an exception of you, he-dog," Sorcha said, wrapping him in a length of flannel and rubbing him a little dry. "You can shelter here tonight."

Brady shivered and whined.

"It *is* cold in the passage. Come with me, then; there are fires in my rooms."

Sorcha let the black dog into her sitting room, and turned from closing the door to find a lanky young man in damp clothes, a towel over his head.

He gave the towel an embarrassed tug as he sank to one knee, his hair hanging in shining black strings.

"Your Grace," he said. "I am your most humble servant."

"I am no monarch. I'm a Wayfarer; nothing more. I don't even know you, varier. …Do I?"

"I owe your sister my life."

"Karol?" Sorcha crouched before the boy, taking his shoulders in her roughened hands. "You know where she is? By the Heart of the Way, don't tell me." She looked behind her at the closed door and spoke more softly. "If you know where Karol is, boy, run away. As fast and as far as you can. Layounna is no place for servants and friends of Onagros." After another look at the door and one at the window, Sorcha lowered her voice again and said, "Karol is alive?"

Brady shook his head. "Dead ten years, but I only knew it when I saw you, Your Grace."

"Don't call me 'Your Grace.' What do you mean, 'Dead ten years'?"

"Ten years ago, a woman came between me and death. She traded her life for mine. You look just like her."

Sorcha's grip tightened on Brady's shoulders. "Tell me."

"It's a long and rambling story, Your Grace. A lot of long and rambling stories. If I'm putting you in danger being here, don't get me started. Just tell me how to serve you."

"Don't call me 'Your Grace,' and leave. Serve me thus."

"It's true, then? You reject the throne?"

"Are you tempting me? Testing me? Who sent you? Corvina?" Sorcha stood, fingering her pendant and scowling at the kneeling boy. "I don't want the throne," she said, the statement sounding sincere out of habit. "Go back and tell your mistress that."

"Corvina is not my mistress. I came here to serve you. I'm on a quest and you're part of it somehow, you and your House."

"I have no House but this Waystation."

Brady grew tired of kneeling, and curled his legs around to sit, tailor-fashion, on the floor. "Where I come from, mothers tell tales of the Wild Dog. The Wild Dog snatches the scraps no one wants – do you follow me?"

Sorcha shook her head.

"Honor what you love, or the Wild Dog will think your treasure is an unwanted scrap and will snatch it away from you. That's what my mother always said. Be certain what you want, and be certain what you don't."

"I want to be safe," said Sorcha. "I want to be left alone. I want my family to be safe and left alone. But I'm afraid he won't…. If I were dead, Hayward would be no threat. But the children…."

"I wanted to be safe and left alone, too," said Brady. "My second choice was to have a second choice. You were it."

Sorcha sat in a chair before the fire and absently patted her thigh, as if Brady were still and truly a dog.

Brady smiled at that and scooted closer.

"I want to go home," said Sorcha. "If ten years in exile from the life I loved means nothing to Landry, I might as well go home."

"Go home, then."

Sorcha shook her head. "Not without knowing Hayward's heart. He's kept faith with me all these years. He tells me he loves me, that a place by my side has been worth a place under a dangling sword. I wonder if he means it. Really means it. When the blow falls, will he curse me, or will he still count the cost no matter? If I could draw Landry's fear away from him, would he let it pass, or would he draw it back? Could I protect him? Would he let me?"

Brady nodded. "I can find out."

"I don't think so. How can you? How can you know his true heart? Who is completely honest with another?"

"It happens," said Brady, thinking of an old woman's eyes. "Let the rain slack off a bit, and I'll go."

"In the night?"

"Then, if ever, he'll speak the undressed truth."

Sorcha smiled wearily. "As I have. Do you have a name, boy? Is this your proper form?"

"Yes, to both questions. I'm Brady birn Ilka, and this is my self. That's all I'll say for now, for the sake of other people. Except for this: You've heard of Kinnan-called-beren-Ada?"

"A made-up character, based on a dead rebel. An invention of the people, to frighten Landry for them in stories."

"Your brother, my lady. He's real, and he's alive. I know him."

Sorcha stood and crossed the room with the stride of Kinnan himself. She opened the door, looked up and down the passage, closed the door and locked it. She strode to the window, opened the shutter, leaned into the rain to look as far as she could see, closed the window and shot the bolt. When she turned to Brady, her rain-wet face was closed, as well.

"Choose your words carefully," she whispered. "Tell me again."

"Your mother, Ada beren Cinnie, had a second heart-husband, one she kept secret. She had a son by him. Kinnan."

"I know his claim, or what the stories claim for him. He tried to raise rebellion against Landry."

"He had cause, my lady. He had the right."

"But he disappeared. Landry's men killed him, I thought, except in the people's imaginations."

"No, he lives. And he hasn't given up."

"Then I was right. I am in danger. Any place that shelters me is in danger."

"Not from Kinnan."

"From Landry. Whenever he feels threatened, he kills someone. If he can't kill who threatens him, he kills who he can reach."

Sorcha faced her own mortal danger, yet she revealed no fear by gesture or expression. Brady had seen such courage before. Once before.

"The sooner I go, then, the sooner you'll know what to do. Or what not to do, as the case may be."

He unbolted and opened the window. A black owl flapped into the downpour, and Sorcha reluctantly closed the shutter behind it.

Hayward Oliva beren Ada sat before his bedroom fire. A window, set in a deep niche and sheltered from the rain by a low eve, stood open. Wind gusted in, bringing splatters of heavy rain with it, some drops reaching halfway across the stone floor. Hayward shivered, but still sat facing the night, letting the drafts swirl around him. He wore a plain woolen nightshirt, and rabbit-fur slippers laced above his ankles. His hands were cold, his face was cold, his nose and cheeks were dusty rose against his olive skin.

He slept through the night less and less often. Night after night he woke and stretched out his hand, and felt a pang of panic when Sorcha wasn't there. It had been ten years since Sorcha had slept beside him, but her absence was stranger and more disorienting every night.

Hayward heard a flutter of wings and saw a large black owl, wet feathers glistening in the firelight, perched on his windowsill.

"Who-oo," the owl hooted.

Hayward put a courtly hand on his heart and dipped his head. "Hayward Oliva beren Ada, bailiff and younger son of the house of Sarpa," he said.

The owl dropped from the sill and landed as a dog.

"Ah, I'm dreaming," said Hayward. He felt more at ease, knowing he was dreaming; sleep was the only freedom he knew.

The dog lay down near the fire, its eyes on the man's face. Brady was tired of being wet, and the dry heat from the fire and the stone hearth felt wonderful. He was content, for a time, to share a companionable silence while he tried to take Hayward's measure from his face.

Hayward thought the dream dog's eyes were almost human, fixed on him but half-closed, calmly watchful, like the eyes of a careful bailiff or a knowing mother. Hayward drew breath to share a true thought, then let it out in a sigh. He closed his eyes and dozed.

Brady turned and stretched until he was completely dry. *Now what?* He might hear this man's confidences if he had a month or two to spare. Then again, he might not. If a man wouldn't unburden himself in the middle of a rainy night to a dog in a dream, what would make him speak?

Hayward stirred. Brady changed himself to the image of Landry Oliva beren Ada and sat in the empty chair across the hearth from Hayward. He made his image waver and reform as Hayward's eyes opened, and often after that; he didn't want Hayward to believe Landry had really come to call.

"Even in my dreams…," said Hayward. "Get out of my dream."

"Brother," said Landry/Brady. "I would know your heart."

"You know it already."

"I do. Better than you think. Your wife–"

"I have no wife. My wife abandoned me rather than do our Kinninger's bidding – your bidding. She took my children, the future of my blood, as surely as if she had drowned them, when she took them into the cloister. Don't speak to me of her."

"Suppose I would avenge you. Suppose I mistrusted the honesty of her withdrawal."

"Oh, she's withdrawn. The woman who lives in the Waystation is no more to me than any other wayfarer."

"And your revenge?"

"It doesn't matter. Hardly a Kinninger's affair, at any rate."

"This coldness isn't like you, brother," Brady guessed.

"You asked for my heart – you have it. You asked about my wife – I told you."

Hayward's gaze was growing sharper; he would soon challenge the unreality of what he saw, and know he wasn't dreaming.

Brady shifted again and held this shape clearly – a mirror image of Hayward: pudgy and chin-heavy, night-shirted and slipper-footed. Only his expression was different. Brady's Hayward wore the weary, friendless look Landry's vision had driven into hiding.

Hayward looked at himself and wept. "Sorcha…. Sorcha…."

"What shall I do?" asked Hayward/Brady.

"She isn't safe," said Hayward.

"She would do anything, go anywhere, to keep me safe," said Brady.

"She's done enough, and it still isn't enough – for *him*," said Hayward. He thumped a plump fist on the arm of his chair. "But would she come with me? Would she let me fight to keep her safe?"

"How?" Brady asked. "Could we oppose the whole realm?"

Hayward laughed at "himself." "We could oppose the whole of the realm that Landry could command against us. That number lessens every day. We could go to Oakwood."

Brady, who didn't know where or what Oakwood was, said nothing.

Hayward laughed again. "Grandmoder longs for Sorcha and treats Blaine and his children as her lineage, even though they're no longer in our line by law. She's never missed visiting Sorcha on her anniversary date. She barely acknowledges Moder as her own, and won't speak Corvina's or Landry's names. She would take us in."

"It would mean treason. That's what Landry would call it. Treason is what our mother would call it."

Hayward shook his head. "*She* wouldn't. Landry has no children. If I take Sorcha out of cloister, have her renounce her abdication, I'll have offspring to carry on our line. Besides personal power, that's what my mother longs for most. Corvina…. She would say, 'Let them weaken each other to my advantage.' They might talk against me to each other and in Landry's ear, but they would be no danger to me. In fact, they would be my agents without my asking."

"And if Landry is deposed?"

"Sorcha can take the throne and use me and my family any way she pleases."

"And if she really doesn't want the throne?"

"Someone will want it. Someone always does. Sorcha can decide. It's her decision. But…."

"Will she come?" Brady finished.

"Will she come?" said Hayward. "She ran from me before. Can I make her see the danger? Can I make her see that the safest place is in the open, now?"

Brady turned into Sorcha, wavering again. Untouchable.

"This is a vision," said Hayward. "Is it true, or one of my mother's?"

"What does it matter?" Sorcha/Brady said. "Truth is truth, even from a liar's mouth. Go to Oakwood. I'll meet you on the road. We'll be safe inside before Landry knows we're going."

"Today," said Hayward. "I was going next week for my quarterly inspection. I'll go today, as soon as riders can be sent to notify the manor. I'll say it's because of the rain. I'll say I might as well go while it's wet, and save the field work for good weather. I'll leave this afternoon. The path comes nearest to the Station back by that group of three cherry trees with their branches intertwined – you know the ones."

Brady didn't, but he made Sorcha nod. "This afternoon."

As a dog, he ran across the puddled patch of floor to the window embrasure. He leapt and, as an owl, flew into the night.

Hayward stumbled to bed and slept without memorable dreams, one hand on the empty place beside him.

Sorcha, half-dozing by her own fire, opened to the owl's scratch and quiet call.

Brady was standing on the hearth before Sorcha bolted the window.

"If I don't take cold from this, it'll be a wonder beyond anything in Kozabir," he said.

"You found Hayward?"

"I found Hayward."

chapter 13
truth in a tale

"I wish we had something to flavor this with," Nerissa said that evening, over the pan of sizzling fish. "Besides salt, I mean. Onions, maybe. I could grow some—"

Tartarus interrupted, saying, "You ought to think again about my offer—"

"—outside, there, where the dirt's washed—"

"—of lessons. Could come in handy—"

Nerissa spoke louder, "—down from above? You could get me some bulbs; onions grow from bulbs, Old Delia told me—"

"—someday, you never know—"

A third voice joined in, gently, but so unexpected that both stopped talking at once: "You'll do better at that if you take turns. One speaks and the other listens, is the way it usually works."

Nerissa could see nothing but a silhouette in the doorway, framed against the setting sun. She shrank toward Tartarus, though she had only the slightest confidence that he would protect her from slavers.

"What do *you* want?" Tartarus asked the figure, his voice heavy with disgust.

"I don't deserve that look. You're the one who was careless. How many rings would this make?"

The words were meaningless to Nerissa, but she knew who spoke them. "Farukh!"

"There's a girl who knows how to make a fellow feel welcome!" said the storyteller, flinging up his arms as he entered the lean-to.

Nerissa blinked away the glare and smiled at him.

"I might have known you'd show up," said Tartarus. "What do you want?"

"A friendly visit, though I suppose I've come to the wrong place for that." Farukh tipped Nerissa a wink that warmed her heart. "Is there enough fish for me?"

"You can have mine."

"No," said Tartarus.

"There's another piece here," said Nerissa. "He can eat what I already cooked for myself and I'll cook this last one for me."

"That's for our breakfast!"

"Have eggs for breakfast," said Farukh. "Or are you still too lazy to gather them?"

Tartarus might have been alone, for all the response he made.

Farukh grinned and fetched a sack from outside. "I happen to have brought a trifle or two with me, remembering your past hospitality. Oats – we'll have porridge for breakfast."

"We?" asked Tartarus.

"Didn't I say? I'm staying a day or two."

"You aren't."

"Why not?" Nerissa demanded.

Tartarus clapped his wooden plate on the floor and said, "He's one of those I warned you about, girl – spy for a slave-catcher."

For a second – for five seconds – Nerissa wondered if it could be. Farukh went everywhere, was welcome in any palace or hole; if he were a spy, he would be a good one. Then she said, "He is not."

Farukh laughed and sat. "Good for you, child. And I'm glad to see you got away from your keepers after all, in spite of Tortoise."

Nerissa blushed at her former gullibility.

Tartarus snorted. "She doesn't believe in Tortoise," he said, mincingly.

"Oh," Farukh said to the girl, "Tortoise is real. As real as Tartarus, here. Where I come from, the ancients believed that the world balanced on Tortoise's back as he swam through the sea of time. They said Tortoise caused the seasons by swimming closer to the sun or farther from it. They said he caused droughts by crawling out of the ocean, and floods by diving down into it. He doesn't like for people to be too comfortable, you see."

"Comfortable people are smug and dull," said Tartarus. "I agree with him on that. Trouble – that's what people need. Most people are worthless without trouble. For instance, take Nerissa, here. She has a dainty taste in fish, but she's going to be eating charcoal for supper *if she doesn't pay attention!*"

Nerissa took the pan off the fire just as the sizzle turned to scorch. "Perfect," she said, answering Tartarus' jeer with a defiant thrust of her chin. "Would you like it, Farukh?"

"That one's yours, girl," said Tartarus.

"He can have it."

"Give it to *me*, if you don't want it."

"No!"

Farukh laughed. "Your latest apprentice is less tractable than most."

"She's none of your business. Eat your fish, girl."

Farukh shook his head at the offered dish, and Nerissa ate.

"Shall I tell you a story about Tortoise?" the storyteller asked, when she was done.

Nerissa nodded, her heart thudding with joy. This would be the first complete story she had ever heard from Farukh. And all for her. Only for her. (Tartarus hardly counted.)

"I'll tell you two. One is true and one is false. You tell me which is which."

Nerissa wiped her mouth on her arm, her hands on the skirt of her ragged dress.

Farukh began:

~*~

Once, my child, there were a brother and sister. The sister was your age; the brother, a year or two older. Now, these children were neither more nor less naughty than most, but one night.... One night, the brother heard the girl crying in terror and woke to see Tortoise crawling across the floor toward her.

"Stop!" the boy shouted.

"The girl is mine," said Tortoise (for, being a Spirit Animal, he could speak).

"Of course," said the boy. "But I happen to know that my sister has a full day of mischief planned tomorrow. Why take a little nip now, when you can wait and take a good big mouthful tomorrow night?"

"I'm hungry now," Tortoise whined.

"Here's a piece of fish I was saving for my breakfast," said the boy, and Tortoise ate it and went away.

~*~

Nerissa laughed and hugged her knees.

~*~

The next day, the sister really was a most shocking child, just as her brother had promised. That night, before she went to bed, the little girl's brother rubbed salt all over her left foot and told her to leave it sticking out of the covers.

When Tortoise came, he took that salty foot in his mouth and the salt rubbed all over his tongue. He pulled back.

"What's the matter?" asked the boy.

"This is the saltiest child I ever tasted," said Tortoise. "Give me something to drink."

The boy had a jug of wine he had told his sister to steal, and he gave it to Tortoise. Greedy as he is, he drained the whole bottle in one swig!

Then, of course, he had to close his eyes for a little nap.

"Quick," said the boy to his sister. "Hide behind that chair and give me your dress."

The boy put his sister's dress on Tortoise's tail.

"Wake up!" the boy cried. "She's trying to get away! She's behind you!"

Tortoise woke up, hissed, and took one angry nip after another – out of his own tail!

~*~

Nerissa let go of her knees and held her sides, hooting with laughter.

"And that is why," said Farukh, "Tortoise's tail has a series of spikes on it: They aren't really spikes, they're all that's left after he got through with himself. They say the little girl was more careful after that. And so, perhaps, was Tortoise."

Nerissa clapped her hands until they were red.

"She'd be better off getting her rest than listening to that trash," said Tartarus.

"Now the other one!" said Nerissa. She realized what she had done – demanding, when she should have been imploring – and hung her head. She felt a hand laid softly on her crown, stroking her greasy hair, and she looked up into Farukh's sparkling blue eyes.

"I know who you've been keeping company with," he said, with his quick, bright smile. "I make allowances."

"Will you tell the other one?" she asked.

"Bah!" said Tartarus. "Why don't you get down on your belly and beg him, girl?"

Nerissa's hand went to the handle of the skillet beside her. Tartarus saw it and gave an evil grin. She let go and, lifting her nose into the air, turned away from him and back to Farukh.

"Please tell me the other one," she said.

"The other one…. It isn't pretty, child. It isn't funny."

But it was, Nerissa felt, important.

"Please," she said.

~*~

Yesterday – or was it a long time ago? – a sword was forged by a very special smith. He was a man born, as all men are, of a man and a woman, but he had from birth a strong communion with making and with metal. A sword of this smith's making was bought by a mercenary, who called the sword a "she" and named her Freer of Souls.

Now you may know, child, that Tortoise is the patron of mercenaries. You may also know that Tortoise loves a sacrifice. To Tortoise, then, was Freer of Souls dedicated, and every life she took was called a sacrifice to him. In return for these gifts, the mercenary asked victory in combat.

After some years, the mercenary began to place himself in the thickest of any battle, to search for assignments that promised to be bloodiest, to give deliberate offense in order to goad other men to fight.

Then, during a border skirmish with another country, this mercenary found himself standing amid the dead and dying of his enemies, and among the more lightly wounded.

"For Tortoise," he said, and proceeded to kill all the helpless living within his reach. When he was done, he moved and began again.

Suddenly, with no puff of smoke, no spark, no rush of wind, the Black Warrior stood before him.

~*~

Nerissa shivered. She had lost sight of the shack, of the dying sun outside, of the storyteller himself. What she saw was a field of murdered men, one man standing among them with a dripping sword, and a soldier in gleaming black armor facing him.

~*~

Do you know the Black Warrior, child? He is Tortoise when he takes a personal hand in a fight.

"This is for you, My Lord," said the mercenary. "Grant me glory. Grant me power."

The Black Warrior raised his sword. "Defend yourself, slayer of wounded."

"But this is for you!"

"Defend yourself. Force your claims against me."

"Grant me nothing, then, but accept my offering."

"A battle bravely fought is an offering to my taste," said the Black Warrior. "Murder never was."

And, while the mercenary faced the Warrior, who was invisible to all but him, a man in the pay of the other country struck, and the mercenary from Granitz fell dead. The victor took Freer of Souls, cleaned her on her dead master's tunic, and replaced his own sword with her. He gave her another name, and he used her more direly than her first owner ever had.

He didn't dedicate his killings to Tortoise, though, so Tortoise took no notice, but left him to fashion his own destruction.

Farukh sat back. "Now," he said, "which story was real, and which was false?"

Nerissa shook herself, feeling as if wisps of narrative still clung about her.

Behind her, Tartarus poked up the fire. "I'm not lighting the lamp." He closed the door on the night. "I've heard enough codswallop for one evening."

"Well, child?" said Farukh.

"The second one is true. The second one."

"Thought you didn't believe," Tartarus mocked.

"I believe the second one."

"Why?" asked Farukh.

"Tortoise, in the second one…. He isn't a fool. He's terrible, but he isn't a monster. And he doesn't belong to anybody."

Tartarus grunted in the darkness. "The girl isn't a total idiot," he said.

"Aren't you going fishing today?" asked Farukh the next morning.

Tartarus licked a last gob of porridge off his forearm and said, "Suppose you come with me?"

Farukh ran his fingers through his short yellow beard, working out tangles and shaping it into a neat point. "I thought I would stay here today. Help Nerissa with her work. Look around."

"It's pretty Up There," Nerissa said, excited at the thought of having her friend all to herself all day. "I could show you. Maybe you know the names—"

"Suit yourself," said Tartarus. "She has a wild cat she feeds. Better watch out for it: It bites."

"He didn't bite hard," Nerissa protested.

"But it bit!" Tartarus shouted, standing up, face red, fists clenched.

Nerissa admitted that he bit, not afraid of Tartarus' sudden anger, but puzzled by it. She was puzzled, too, at Farukh's smothered chuckles.

Tartarus kicked his bowl, sending it skittering across the floor.

"He's a nasty cat," Nerissa told Farukh, gauging Tartarus' reaction out of the corner of her eye. "He's dirty and he's mean."

Tartarus seemed placated by this, but Nerissa couldn't help adding, "I like the poor old thing, though."

Farukh broke into laughter as another man might break into song. When he had finished, he said, "I think I will go fishing, after all."

"I'll take these down to wash now, before the porridge gets hard." Nerissa gathered the bowls and spoons and fled. She knew she couldn't hide her disappointment at Farukh's change of plans, and she knew Tartarus would mock her melancholy.

Trying to look as if she didn't care, she watched the men cross the beach, dragging the coracle behind them. She waved back at the storyteller as Tartarus' powerful oarstrokes pulled the little boat out of the bay and out of sight.

The world seemed empty, now that Farukh had come and gone. The sun seemed dull, though oppressively hot. Nerissa took the sand-scoured, salt-rinsed dishes back to the lean-to, folded herself into her bedcloths, and went back to sleep.

She slept until the sun was low. She woke abruptly – Tartarus would be returning, and Farukh would be with him. The ugly feeling of the morning had vanished; now she wanted to be on the beach when the coracle came in sight, to wring every drop of the storyteller's presence from his visit.

What if Farukh isn't with him? she asked herself, as she scrambled down to the sand. *What if he's driven him away, or put him out somewhere?* She could envision Tartarus rowing away from shore, answering Farukh's demands or pleas with nothing but his evil grin. Somehow, though, she couldn't see Farukh demanding or pleading – or allowing himself to be stranded.

No boat in sight yet. Nerissa looked around for "her" cat, feeling a bit guilty at having slept through their time together. No sign of him now, though, and she had an unfounded feeling he hadn't come at all.

The coracle slid into view. Farukh raised a hand. Tartarus hunched more over his oars.

Nerissa jumped up and down, waving both arms above her head.

"Hello! Hello-o-o!" she called.

Tartarus splashed out of the coracle before it grounded and pulled it with Farukh still inside, tipping it as he tugged. With a laugh, Farukh steadied himself and leapt clear before he tumbled out into the water.

"Did you have a nice day?" Nerissa asked Farukh. "Did you catch any fish?"

"Too busy talking, as usual," said Tartarus. He flung the net bag of his catch to Nerissa. "Here. Three, today." He flapped Farukh on the sleeve with the back of one hand and said, "Come on."

"I thought I'd stay and—"

"Leave her alone. You promised." Tartarus' wicked grin blossomed in the black tangle of his beard. "Or break your promise. I could live with you breaking your word."

"My word can still be trusted," said Farukh. With the grimmest look Nerissa had ever seen on his face, he said, "He's clever. Had you noticed?"

"No," said Nerissa, furious at Tartarus' interference and at Farukh's compliance with it.

It was a prickly evening. Farukh tried to smooth it, but Nerissa seemed to have caught Tartarus' sour spirit and refused to be either entertained or charmed.

At last, feigning weariness, Nerissa rolled herself into her rags and affected sleep.

She heard Farukh and Tartarus move out into the night. She heard them sit just outside the door.

"You might as well move along," Tartarus said.

"Yes, I think you're right."

"No use waiting till morning. I won't change my mind in the night."

"I harbor no such hope, my brother. I know you too well. Better than you think, perhaps."

"Pity you learned too late." Tartarus chuckled unpleasantly.

Farukh made no reply.

"You aren't going to argue anymore?" Nerissa thought she heard a note of frustrated challenge in Tartarus' question.

"Sorry, but no. There's no point, is there?"

"Well," said Tartarus, sounding let down, like a gambler when the game is over. "What'll we contend for next, I wonder?"

"People weren't made to be playing pieces! This hasn't been a contest. There won't be any prize. You don't *win*." Farukh's voice came louder, clearer. Nerissa imagined him turning to look in at her as he said, "That isn't a stone, it's a child. A living child. If shame weren't foreign to you, you'd be ashamed. The blood of the future is on you. Can you smell it? Can you feel it steam?"

After too long a pause, Tartarus said, "Very colorful. Nice visit. Come again."

Nerissa wanted to leap up, cling to the storyteller, beg him to take her with him, but she felt that this would compromise his promise, somehow. Instead, she lay still and listened to him gather his things. She steadied her breathing and kept her eyes closed as he bent over her with a gentle touch on her cheek. She held her tears tight as she listened to him climb the bluff to the spring and the berries and the flowers above.

Tartarus came in, closing and latching the door. He stood over her a moment, muttered, "Living child. Steaming blood." He grunted. "Wordsmith!"

Nerissa stirred as if waking, and he blew out the light and shuffled to his own pallet.

chapter 14
master of the sword

Guthrie was half afraid to buckle Deya on again, as if she would sense and resent his bid for escape.

Could Oliva free him from Deya's demands? Oliva's plan, but his own action? He was to do the work of finding this smith of wonders, he was to do the work of bringing him to Kudasad, and of finding and slaying the unicorn – slaying it or capturing it. And Oliva would profit from the beast or from its remains.

Guthrie had long since stopped searching for his own mother, except in hope among the dead. And yet, when he saw that wren of a woman stand with trembling courage before her regal son… when she turned to her son's Chief Sword with comfort though she, herself, still shook from Landry's forcefulness… when she shared private glances with him, as a mother does with a privileged child…. At these times, Guthrie felt his loyalty to Landry shift to Oliva beren Audre. The feeling frightened and excited him.

He felt the same, now, as he reached for his sword. He picked her up. She felt warmer than ever, as if all the life she'd stolen since her forging heated her from within.

She knows. She wants the blood of the unicorn. She wants that dousing. I'll have myself back, and Deya in my debt.

And Thane Oliva. The success of this quest would buy a place at her side, a place at Corvina's side.

The prospect of becoming Corvina's bridegroom stirred no longing in him and no delight – except that it would be a place of power. And, Guthrie admitted as he saddled his horse, except that it would make him part of the House of Sarpa. He would share the household of the Kinninger himself! He would share his matronym! Thane Oliva would call him "son."

Guthrie Melanell beren Oliva – He tested the name in his mind. It sounded natural. It sounded right. It was a name written on the Shining Path of the Way by a Divine hand.

And then the mighty Chamberlain, speaker of foreign tongues and maker of treaties, would see who was a jackal and who was a lion. He would bow and admit that Guthrie had seized success where he, Rhu beren Robia, had met with dismal failure. The prospect was sweet. When he returned in triumph to marriage with the Kinninger's sister, to elevation into the House of Sarpa, and to Oliva and Landry's gratitude, he would treat himself to the satisfaction of cracking the Chamberlain's mockingly courteous gloss, if not – here was a lovely thought – his bones.

The Sword rode hard to Granitz, his head clearer than it had been for years. He felt young again. He slept without dreams.

Guthrie rode into Kozabir's capital with the last rays of the setting sun, when the shops and bazaars were dark and the inns and taverns gleamed. He would have preferred to pretend he spoke no Kozabiri, to see what information he could gather if people thought they needn't guard their speech. Unfortunately, his mission depended on conversation and on making himself known. The guards bantered with him, thanks to his uniform, as comrades-in-arms, but he sensed a reserve and a resentment in them. A soldier of a border dispute's winning side expected that from the losers.

"What brings you to Grantiz?" the Captain of the guards asked, as if in friendship.

"I bring an offer of business for one of your craftsmen, if I can find him."

"Who is it? One of us may know him."

It was quizzing well done, but Guthrie had performed enough interrogations to know one. Still, he had nothing but his ultimate purpose to hide, and that was easily hidden.

"I don't know his name. I'm looking for the man who made my sword. Do I have your permission to draw her?"

"'Her,' is it? Raise your hands. I'll draw 'her.'"

Guthrie forced his hands away from Deya's pommel and suffered another man to touch her, to slide her from her sheath.

For the first time, Guthrie felt how easily she would pass from his hands to another's. He remembered how he had felt when he had first wrapped his hands around her hilt: that he had found *his* sword. For the first time, now, he understood that the feeling was not mutual. Deya had no soul, felt no partnership, no loyalty, no joy in his touch. She was a lifeless work of metal. He told himself this, and knew it for a lie. She lived, but she did not live for him, nor for any living creature, but only for herself.

The Captain inspected her and showed her to the men who had just barred the city gate. All shook their heads "no," and the Captain slid Deya into place again.

"Not regulation," the Captain said. "And out of our price range. What did you pay for her?"

"I took her in a trade." His old sword and the blood of her former master, in exchange for this most demanding mistress. His peace and free- dom, in trade for dreadful nights and days of burning want. The Sword's hands clenched on sheath and pommel, pressing his torment back into her proper place. "I thought I'd try a few mercenaries' taverns. One of them might recognize the work."

"I'll come with you. I've just been relieved." The Captain motioned to another soldier, this one wearing a broad red belt, apparently an indication of Officer In Charge. "Leave your horse here, for my men to take care of, and we'll make the rounds together. I could do with a drink. Or two."

Guthrie couldn't refuse the escort. He met the Captain's smile with one of his own, memorizing the man's face, hoping he might meet it one day in battle.

They stopped first at a white-washed lean-to a few hundred yards along the city wall from the gate Guthrie had entered. The Captain was greeted by name – Yogan birn Hilda. No one there had seen anything like Deya, but directed Guthrie to a place closer to the market.

Guthrie and Yogan each pretended to down a full mug of beer and moved on.

Three taverns later, Yogan stopped across a cobble street from a box of a place with a hole-in-corner exterior. Its windows were small and tightly shuttered and its door was firmly closed, but light leaked from every un- stopped chink and keyhole.

"You remember this place, don't you?" Yogan asked. "You've been here before. This is where you thought you'd cornered your rebel, but found you hadn't."

The Sword gritted his teeth in an unconvincing smile. "I do remember.

We were given incorrect information as to the building's exits, or we would have had him."

"Your information would have been correct if you had gotten it from my sources instead of your own."

"I'll remember that, the next time I bring my men here to flush out a traitor." Guthrie laughed. Yogan joined him, eyes glittering coldly, and they crossed the street.

About half the tables were full. Waves and shouts of recognition greeted Yogan, and the soldiers at one table made room for the Captain and his companion. These were not men and women of the guard, but wore whatever clothing they felt most comfortable wearing and whatever armor experience had taught them to favor. Mercenaries, in pay or for hire.

Yogan ordered beer for himself and Guthrie.

"Who's your friend?" one of the men asked. Turning to Guthrie before Yogan could answer, he asked, "From Layounna, aren't you? One of their Swords?"

"Not just 'one,'" said Yogan. "This is Guthrie beren Melanell, the Chief Sword, himself, back to visit us again."

Guthrie could see in the mercenaries' eyes that they remembered his attempt at a capture in another force's territory, and that they remembered his failure with relish.

"You ever catch that rebel of yours?" a woman across the table asked.

"No. He's gone to ground somewhere. Probably passed into lands unknown, or begging his way through the three-shack villages on your northern border."

"Or biding his time," muttered a man lighting a pipe.

"He's been a long time biding," said Guthrie.

"'Tortoise is a long time crawling,'" said the man with the pipe, "'but he gets there, by and by.'"

Guthrie chuckled with the others. "His Grace isn't worried. But it isn't the rebel who brings me here, this time." He asked Yogan, "May I draw my sword here?"

Yogan glanced around the table. The others nodded, and he said, "Slowly, and lay 'her' on the table. Gently."

"Have any of you ever seen this workmanship before?"

Deya stretched along the table, flanked by mugs and tumblers. She was nearly half Guthrie's height in length, her edges crimped so that she did more damage than a smooth blade. Her pommel was made of red wood, darkened to maroon with use; the guard was of blackened metal set with silvery rivets.

Could they feel the pulse of her, Guthrie wondered, as he could? Could they feel the warmth, born of the blood she had drunk, the blood he had grown to covet for her?

The mercenaries exclaimed at the power and elegance of the blade, the simple beauty of the hilt. Several had seen swords something like her, but nothing equal.

Except for one man. "I've seen her match. In fact, unless I miss my memory, I've seen this very sword."

Guthrie's hand closed on Deya's grip. Yogan made a cautionary noise and Guthrie moved his hand away again. "Where?"

"She belonged to a man in a company I fought in once. A particular friend of mine, as a matter of fact. He died in a border skirmish against Layounna. I didn't see him die, but they tell me he was killed where he stood, with this sword in his hand, and that this sword was taken from his body by the man who killed him. A man with red hair, I was told. Layounna is rich in red hair, but I'm thinking you were the man. Am I right?"

"The spoils of war," said Guthrie, his hand poised near Deya's hilt.

The man nodded. "That's right. Glennon would have been the first to grant you that. You're not the only soldier at this table who fights with gear taken in death."

They told tales, then, of battle-won weapons. A woman the others called Koree showed a knife, single-edged, slim, and blue of blade, that she had taken in a battle in Sule.

"Speaking of Sule," she said, "reminds me of that story about the Phoenix armor."

There was a murmur, as those who remembered the tale sketched it for those who did not. Then came a dead stillness Guthrie didn't understand, then another murmur – more muted, this time.

"I'll tell it, shall I?" a man asked. "I heard it in Istok when I was held for ransom by Anshar's Raiders."

"Anshar!" one of the men shouted, and raised his mug. Others echoed the salute. Guthrie did not.

Anshar –"the Divine Spear"– was beginning to make a serious nuisance of himself. He raided across the border between Istok and Layounna, claiming to be a partisan of the rebel, Kinnan. Even worse, he only struck supporters of Landry's rule, and only rich ones, at that. It was a raiding strategy calculated to minimize popular resentment. Guthrie strongly suspected that the locals would have shielded and sheltered the rebels, but he had found no evidence that such assistance had ever been asked.

The man who had volunteered the story was bought a mug of beer by way of encouragement. He drank a third of it at one gulp and rose, resting one foot on his bench and his hand on his raised knee. He was dark-complected, with long black hair that fell in tight curls nearly to his waist. Steel clamps, which had held the curls in a tight knot at the back of his head, gleamed on the table before him. His features were well-formed, but a little on the heavy side. Guthrie felt he knew him, but could not place the remembrance. Perhaps, he thought, they had fought together – or against each other – in some past battle. He wore civilian clothes now, with not so much as a wrist guard by way of armor; if they had met as soldiers, the change of clothing alone would make recognition difficult.

When the man spoke, his voice was smooth and compelling.

~*~

In Istok (he said), they say there are mountains in Sule that spit fire. They say the first bit of fire the first fire-mountain ever spit was Phoenix. As for what it looks like, some stories have it as a hummingbird; others, as a pheasant with five long curling tail feathers. Sometimes, it appears as a peacock, which is why peacock's feathers are supposed to be good luck. And sometimes, they say, it's a creature of flame and brightness, with none of the smoldering control of Istok's beloved dragons. They say it's he and she, a single creature with two natures intertwined. Fire and ash, heat and light, destruction and generation – Two as One and One as Two. They say it can appear as male or female or as both, as bird or as human. In whatever form, the heart of Phoenix burns clear and fierce, and its punishments are impatient. Ever put your hand into a flame? How long did the fire wait to burn you?

Well, they say there was a man, a soldier, who hired himself to fight in the deserts of Sule. In the thick of the battle, a blow to the back of his head felled him, and he was left for dead. When he woke, it was dark, and all was quiet except for the last moans and gasps of the dying. He had been stripped of his armor and his weapons, as had the bodies around him. By moonlight, he examined corpses and the sparse bushes. Finally, half-buried in sand, he found the upper part of a broken lance. With something that could deal death in his hand, the soldier felt at ease and began to think of how he might survive.

He returned to scavenging the dead, hoping to find food. Then he smelled smoke and baking bread. Peering, sniffing, climbing what slight elevations he could find and peering again, he at last sighted a glimmer of flame.

The soldier crept closer, using dunes and stands of thin grasses to cover his approach. Making himself as flat as possible, he wriggled to a spot where he could see the fire and the man who sat beside it.

This man was tall. His fair hair and beard glittered in the firelight, as if they gave off sparks to answer those of the crackling wood. Next to him lay a suit of armor of the kind they make in Nishi: A tunic made of two layers of feather-light ironwood rods, one layer horizontal, one layer vertical, decorated with twists of colored thread and beads of semi-precious stones. Atop the armor rested a long curved blade with a wickedly notched tip, and a small smooth shield.

"I have bread, freshly baked on a stone, Comrade," the fair man said. "I have a flask of water and one of wine, and I have a wallet of jerked meat. Come and join me."

The soldier had no way of knowing if this man who spoke so kindly was an enemy willing to call a truce for the night or a soldier in the same pay as himself. All he knew was that the man had things he wanted and that he would be surely safe if the man were dead. So he rose from his place of surveillance, walked openly up to his host, and drove the lance into the welcomer's throat.

Guthrie felt his hand stretch toward Deya, at the thought of the blood-soaked sand. He remembered Yogan's warning, and clenched his fist.

The soldier (the tale-spinner said) ignored the dead man and the food and drink he had offered and examined the sword and shield. He put them down and took up the armor. It was beautiful, and the stones clacked pleasantly against the wooden rods. He eased the tunic over his head and laced it tight.

The corpse heaved. The murderer snatched up the sword and shield and whirled to face it. It heaved again, but not in life. Once more, and it turned to powdery ash and was drawn into the fire.

As the last of the body vanished, the armor altered: now it was made of balsam and sandalwood, cinnamon and cedar. The threads and stones became fragrant herbs and spices – lavender, mint, rosemary, nutmeg, citronella. And it was warm. And it was hot, my Comrades.

Guthrie had never heard this story, but others had. They answered the black-haired man in a ragged chorus: *Hot! It was hot, my Comrades!*

The man went on: The sword moved itself and struck the shield. Where it struck, a spark flew! A spark flew, and touched the wooden tunic. It flamed! (His eyes wide and wild in the grip of his story, the man raised his arms, his fingers seeming to be fingers of fire as he spoke.)

The soldier shrieked once, but no more, for he was utterly consumed in that scented holocaust. Nothing was left but char in the shape of a man, and the heavy incense of aromatic woods and spices. Then, slowly, the blackened figure moved. As it moved, the charcoal dropped away until a living man rose from the ruins. He was tall. His skin was pink and soft and hairless as a newborn babe's. He stood and stretched (the teller demonstrated) and dressed in fresh clothes from his pack. Then Phoenix ate his meal in privacy and peace.

The crowd applauded. The black-haired man grinned, obviously pleased with his success, and returned to his seat.

Guthrie eased Deya from the table and back into her sheath.

He understood the purpose of the story, why it had been asked for and why the request for it had brought such stillness around him. In spite of their talk of battle spoils, something about his taking of Deya struck them as unfair. True, the man he took her from had not been actively fighting; he had been standing, staring before him as if transfixed by some vision only he could see. But an enemy is an enemy. Guthrie hadn't become Landry's Chief Sword – and retained his position and risen to Oliva's household – by indulging in weak-kneed "courtesy" on or off the field.

"What I want to know," he said, "is where my sword came from. Before your friend had her, I mean. Where she was made. Who made her."

After a pause, one of the women said, "That looks like Trahern's work, to me. Nothing bizarre, but not ordinary, either."

"Where will I find this Trahern?"

"I think he comes from the other side of the Inland Sea, on the edge of the Geiskeflor. They say that's why his things are…a bit uncanny, sometimes."

The Chief Sword allowed himself a smile. "Special work can command a special price. He would thank you for sending me to him."

The woman looked around the table. Her silent question was answered with shrugs and nods.

"He's in Granitz now. I saw him in the Central Plaza yesterday. He'll be there for the rest of the week."

Guthrie thanked the woman and bought a round of drinks for the mercenaries at his table. As soon as they were served and his health had been toasted with apparent but suspect sincerity, he left. Yogan, still protesting concern for a stranger in an unfamiliar town, escorted him to an inn.

When the tavern door had closed on the two, the black-haired talespinner opened it and spat after Guthrie's receding footfalls.

"By my body," he said, closing himself again into the warmth of the tavern, "may a thousand demons howl their red-haired brother to eternal torment."

The curse was widely acclaimed as a good one. "Well said," was the consensus. "Well said, Anshar! Bring it to pass, Anshar, Spear of the Divine Ones."

"Someone will, if I don't," Anshar said. "Such a man with such a sword as that will be lucky if he meets his death by human hands." He raised his mug. "To luck, Brothers and Sisters. To luck."

~*~

"Yes, I made it," said Trahern. The burly smith looked at the sword held, naked, across the Layounnan's palms. "It's one of mine. May I…?"

The smith's eyes narrowed to crinkled slits. He could feel the thrumming of other people's blood through Deya's essence. She was ripe with murder; she was nearly glutted.

Guthrie grinned. "She's seen a lot of use."

"A great deal of use. Are you… dissatisfied?"

Guthrie sheathed her. "I didn't come to complain. I was sent to find her maker. The Kinninger of Layounna has need of his services. If you are the man, I'm to escort you back to Kudasad. You'll be well paid and much honored."

"What do you want me to do? Make more swords like that one? I can't just do it, you know. Sometimes the power goes into the piece, sometimes it doesn't. I don't put it there, you see?"

"No, but My Lady Oliva will. She doesn't want a sword; she wants a bit and bridle."

"A b – I have any number of them, here. Take one."

Guthrie shook his head. "My Lady wants to see you make it."

Trahern felt himself turn stiff under the big red-head's gaze. Layounna – Kudasad – the palace of Kinninger Landry Oliva beren Ada.... He, Kinnan's old friend, in the service of Kinnan's bitterest enemy. "Away from my own place.... Away from the Geisxeflor.... I can't guarantee...."

"My Lady can."

"I'm expecting someone at home," said Trahern. He had been mounting the wagon when he'd stopped, turned back, and placed the lantern on the porch. That meant, he'd come to know, that someone lost and in need – someone connected with Kinnan beren Ada and his honest cause – would be stumbling by, finding his forge by the lantern's piercing light.

Guthrie didn't reply, but stood before Trahern's stall with the pleasant vacancy of someone who knows objections will collapse before him.

Something moved within Trahern. Whether it was a summoning from Oliva, an insistence from Deya, the immovable presence of Deya's "master," or some other urging, Trahern suddenly knew that he would go.

"I'll leave my stall in a friend's care," he said. "I can leave in an hour."

Guthrie smiled with all his teeth, easy and loose and confident. Oliva always knew what she was about. Who could resist Thane Oliva? Who could resist Deya beren Blotha, rich as she was with souls? And, when she was surfeited and satisfied, who could resist the man who wielded her?

chapter 15
memory

Kinnan came through the screen of trees first, holding a branch aside for the woman who followed.

Small, she walked with a girl's grace, a matron's confidence, an old woman's care. Her skin was brown, her eyes an opaque black. Her hair was a mass of salt-and-pepper frizz. She was dressed in swirls and drapes of multi-colored cloth, sewn with mirrors and clicking bangles. Strings of metal baubs dangled from her ears; a jeweled stud twinkled at one side of her nose.

Elsie, still dressed as a peasant boy, rose from her bench outside the cottage door, delight clear on her face. "You must be Salali."

The market-woman laughed. "All the young men are glad to see me. Charm, trinket, bauble or trifle – say what you want and I'll fashion it, be it a gift for your mother or an ornament to please your lady-love." She looked around the clearing and at Moder, who stepped out of the doorway. "A welcoming place."

"There is ever a welcome here for you," said Moder. "And for Farukh."

Kinnan took Salali's arm and led her across the clearing. "I've waited long enough. Give me my news."

Moder Zglaria pointed to the door behind her with the stem of her pipe. "There's the cottage." She waved the stem in a semi-circle. "There's the rest of the island. Where do you want to go to hear your war chat?"

"Here." Kinnan sat on the rim of the well, gesturing for the women to sit together. "Here, with you listening, is the only place I feel safe from being overheard."

Elsie nodded her understanding. Moder puffed her pipe.

Salali sat between the two. "The news, then. First, your resurrection is welcome to the rebels and refugees in Istok. They'll pass it on to other bands. Some of the leaders are old comrades of yours, and told me to tell you they're ready – now – to add their handfuls to your army."

"Army? What army?"

"The army that will rise the moment you call for one. The people are ready, too."

"Ready for blood and slaughter," said Moder Zglaria. "Ready for revenge and reprisals. The throne must be precious, indeed, Young Master."

Elsie shuddered.

"You said you believed in me," said Kinnan.

"And have I said I don't?"

"The country is mine by right. You can trust me to use it better than Landry has."

"Whatever's left of it."

"Force is the only way. I know war is terrible – I've fought before; I've seen it. I don't want it. But it's the only way."

"Perhaps it is." Moder extended her cane to rub the back of a passing goat. It bleated thanks and trotted away, raising tiny dust storms in the patchy yard.

"Go on," Kinnan said to Salali.

"One of the leaders – Anshar, of the Istok raiders – would have come with me, gathering the army as we came. I said he had better wait." She looked at Moder, as if she asked approval.

"I don't recall an Anshar," Kinnan said.

"He told me to tell you he's appointed himself your chief lieutenant."

"Has he? And can I trust him to stay happy as a chief lieutenant?"

"Until Landry is deposed, certainly. For now, you can trust him. Better: You can be grateful to him. He's winning you friends, taking his risks in your name."

"What other news?" said Kinnan.

"Some messages from old friends in the raider camps. Greetings and remembrances; fireside talk for later."

"Anything else?"

"Landry has trotted out some ancient tale about a mandate bag–"

"It isn't just a tale," said Kinnan. "My mother's family ruled by the right of their subjects' consent, and the bag was the sign of it." He pulled out and unwrapped the glittering pouch he carried and turned it in the sun, flashing rainbows over the ground and walls, half-blinding himself and the women. "This is mine. I bought some amber in Pazni, and an ebony ring set with chips of diamond, ruby, and sapphire. I even have…," he closed his hands around the bag, "…two shreds of alicorn. What does Landry claim? That he has Karol's bag?"

"No, no. That would just be something else for the people to say he'd stolen. He claims the House of Onagros lost its mandate. He's made his own bag, and plans a ceremony – he'll offer it to citizens who'll beg him to keep it and rule."

"When?"

"Midsummer Eve."

"So soon? Little more than a month!"

"You needn't hurry," Moder said. "A sack of baubles handed to him by creatures of his own won't make Landry rightful, no matter what his mother tells him."

Kinnan folded his mandate into its wrapping and stowed it away.

"Speaking of his mother," Salali said, "brings me to Elsie."

"To me?"

"No, Little Master." The market woman turned to the "boy" next to her and spoke with conscious clarity. "I said 'Elsie,' not 'Edelin.' Elsie beren Devona, the Kinninger's new bride. Have you heard about that here?"

Moder Zglaria smiled broadly. "Oh yes."

"They know *all* about her." Kinnan smiled, too, looking younger without his customary sullen determination.

"She has yet to make an appearance. Landry is still saying she's in the castle, too ill to be seen. He says he hasn't taken his new married name because the bride fell ill before the marriage could be finalized. Her father says he's visited her, and she's being cared for royally. Her mother won't go near the castle grounds."

Elsie leaned against the cottage wall and laughed, hugging herself as if she held a memory strong enough to feel. "He *would* say that. She *would* refuse."

Moder spoke to Kinnan. "She remembers." She showed her own white, blocky teeth, sharing Elsie's pleasure.

"I remember?" said Salali.

"Elsie remembers." He waved a hand at Elsie, as if he were producing her from nowhere. "This is Landry's bride."

Salali, too surprised for courtesy, pointed to "Edelin" as if at an object and said, "This?"

"A good disguise, isn't it?" said Moder. "You'd be astonished at who it's fooled."

"Does the young one know where you are?" Salali asked, remembering Brady's face as he spoke of Elsie, astray in the Geiskeflor. "The one who lost you?"

"He knew her at once," Kinnan admitted. "We found her here. As if she'd been waiting for me."

"Waiting for you?" Elsie remained leaning against the wall, at ease, loose and peaceful. "What do you mean?"

"You can give Landry's tale the lie. You can ride with me, or write as much of your story as you want to tell, and I can carry that."

She shook her head. "That's Brady's story more than mine. He might not want it told in public."

"He doesn't seem shy, to me."

"No, but he is a little devious. Just a little."

Moder grunted a laugh.

"Better to leave them out of it," said Salali. "The people believe Landry's lying, as it is. It serves your purpose better to have them think the girl is in the castle. If they know she's safe, they won't be as ready to storm the bailey with you."

"Lie to my people? Begin my leadership by lying to them?"

"This is how it's done," Salali said, apologetically.

"Not by a beren Ada." Behind him, deep within the well, the waters stirred. "We'll wait for Brady, and ask if he'll let me tell his story – I don't dare hope he'll come on the campaign with me." To Moder, he said, "When can we expect him?"

The old woman shrugged. "He went on an errand for me, but I don't know where it led him and I don't know how long he'll be away."

"He will come back?" said Elsie.

"By and by. If he can."

"Meanwhile," Kinnan said, "suppose Salali went back and brought me my 'lieutenant'? Could this be our headquarters?"

Elsie shot to her feet, all but flew across the yard, and clutched Kinnan's tunic in both her fists. The fury on her face shocked him backward; only her grip kept him from tumbling into the well.

"Keep it out of Fiddlewood! Keep your blood and glory out of here! – They'll find it!" She shook the man's clothing, trying to shake the man. "They'll kill it! I remember what it said: the hunters will find it through me!" She looked around, wildly, as if she might see the thing she feared – or the thing for which she feared – beside her.

Kinnan put his big hands over Elsie's slender ones. "Find what? What hunters?"

Elsie released her grip and stood, her hands in Kinnan's. "The...hunters.... Rhu...." She looked at Moder Zglaria. "Rhu beren Robia was here, looking for it.... Looking for me."

"Keep thinking," Moder said.

A look of tenderness Rhu beren Robia would have given much to see softened Elsie's eyes and mouth. "He didn't want to find it. Or me. He said...he loves me."

"The Chamberlain?" Salali said. "That stone-face?"

Elsie turned on her, and Salali chuckled kindly.

"I take it back. I've never seen him show a flicker of emotion. But, then...." Her eyes lost their amusement. "I'm just an old market woman."

"Elsie." Kinnan jogged the hands he held. "What 'it' are you talking about?"

"The unicorn. I remember it clearly, now. I met it in the woods – the one you saw." She raised her head. "Tremendous. Beautiful!"

"One of us must have seen it wrong. This was monstrous."

"But beautiful!" Elsie insisted. "Just because it doesn't look like what it isn't.... How could you not see how beautiful it is?"'"

Salali sat forward on the bench. "Tell me about it."

"I...can't. The more I remember, the less I can tell."

Salali nodded. "They say that's the way of it."

"You wouldn't want to meet it," Kinnan said.

"It isn't pretty," Moder explained.

Salali nodded again, with satisfaction. "That's what they say. In my country, they call it 'the White Tiger.' They say it appears out of nowhere and strikes without warning. They say only purity is absolutely safe from it, but it is its own judge of who's pure and who isn't."

Elsie spoke to Kinnan, her fury gone, but her manner solemn and intense: "We have to protect it."

"It didn't look like it would need much protecting. I don't think it gets in trouble very often."

Elsie turned to Moder Zglaria for support.

The old woman cocked her head as if her question were sincere: "How often does something have to get in trouble to warrant your protection, Young Master?" Before he could answer, she said, "A revolution's headquarters is in the hearts of the people. If it isn't there, it isn't anywhere. Better to keep on the move, when you move against Sarpa."

"That's true." Kinnan released Elsie's hands. "All right, Kitten. If the fight comes to Fiddlewood, it won't be me that brings it."

~*~

Later, after supper had been cleared away, Moder and Elsie fed the stock and tucked them up for the night while Kinnan and Salali spoke of old companions and revolt.

When that was done and the four were grouped around the fire with cups of hot spearmint tea, Elsie said, "Who'd like to tell a story?"

"How about you?" Kinnan asked Moder Zglaria.

"A story from me?"

Kinnan felt himself flush, and told himself it was from the tea, but knew it was a form of panic. Now that he had asked, he wasn't sure he wanted to hear a story from this particular teller. He wasn't sure what he thought he might be in for, but he was certain it would be more than an evening's entertainment.

"Once upon a time," Moder said, "there was a badger who wanted to be emperor of the world."

Kinnan scowled.

Moder cocked an eyebrow. "I see you know that one. Well, perhaps our Mistress Elsie would favor us with a tale. What do you say to it, girl?"

"Oh," said Elsie, shaking her head, "I don't know any...." She stopped abruptly, and her eyes grew dreamy. After a pause the length of three deep breaths, she began:

~*~

Once there was a little girl who lost her past and found it, lost it and found it again.

She was called "Tabby," because it was said – with fondness – she was as lazy as a cat.

Tabby lived on a baby farm, not the oldest nor the youngest of the children there. She helped with the work, in the house and in the garden, and she loved to bring the cow into the shed and to collect eggs from the hens' nests and to watch the bees.

The first thing Tabby could remember was an occasion of great excitement. The house was swept and garnished with sweet-smelling plants, the children's simple clothes were washed and hung over bay bushes to dry in the sun, and the children were coached by the farm's Moder in the elements of courtesy. These mainly consisted of bowing and curtseying, and of not speaking unless they were spoken to.

Late in the morning, when all was ready and the children had just begun to fidget the crispness off their clothes, a host of people rode up to the door.

Everyone rushed to the windows to see the arrival. It wasn't unusual for kind people from a nearby town to come with material for clothing, or donations of food or playthings. It wasn't very unusual for someone to come with an eye to selecting a foster child or an apprentice. This, though – this was different.

There were many men and women on horseback, all dressed in rich cloth and glittering with jewels. Tabby thought they must be creatures out of the tales Moder told them before bed. There was a wagon with a roof, and walls of golden gauze. While the children watched, open-mouthed, one of the men dismounted and pulled a set of steps from the back of the wagon. He held out his hand and helped a woman climb down.

Tabby thought she was the most beautiful woman on earth, her red-brown hair gleaming copper in the sunlight.

The next thing Tabby remembered, she was standing before the beautiful woman, who was sitting in Moder's chair. The woman smiled at her and asked, "Do you know who I am?"

"Yes," she remembered saying. "Your name is Grace."

She remembered how everyone laughed at that, and how shocked and furious she was at them for laughing – she was certain she had been told the woman was called Grace. She never forgot the hot shame she felt at her mistake.

The woman, though, lifted her into her lap and said, "Well spoken. I am sometimes called 'Grace.'" The woman hugged her tightly and put her down.

All the people carried bouquets of purple sage blossoms tied in white ribbon. "Grace" untied hers and gave each child a sprig to remember her by.

After the visitors had gone, Tabby found the ribbon from the woman's bouquet under the table. One of the older children tried to take it from her, but Moder told them no, the ribbon belonged to Tabby. She kept it tied to her bedpost or, sometimes, around her wrist, and stroked it every night and every morning.

~*~

Kinnan laughed, joy and love softening his hardened features and loosening his tense joints. "That's my sister. The visitor was Her Grace, Kinninger Karol beren Ada. That's so like her – to care more for a child's feelings than the amusement of the court. As I should know. I thank you for that story. I'll treasure it, the way Tabby treasured that ribbon."

"She isn't finished," said Moder.

Elsie, still lost in her narrative, did not reply, but continued:

~*~

One day – she never knew how much later, but it was after Old Moder Caitlin left and the young Moder Masheva came to stay – Grace came back. She was dressed in rags, but Tabby knew her and shouted hello. All the children ran to her, to see the baby she held in her arms. Grace left, but the baby stayed. Gosling, it was called, and Tabby doted on it. The children told Moder about Grace's earlier visit, with the gold-gauze wagon and the gentlemen and ladies, but Moder only laughed and kissed them and praised their invention.

Then….

~*~

Elsie stopped speaking. Her face grew pale and a muscle in her jaw tensed. She started to speak, but no sound came out.

Moder Zglaria, in a softer tone than she commonly used, said, "Pass that part by, for now. This is the first loss, I think."

Elsie said, hoarsely, "It's part of the story."

"Good girl," said Moder. She spoke very quietly, the words resting on silence like blessings on a withered soul. "Brave girl."

~*~

A cramp in her leg saved Tabby's life.

That year – the year she was four – her muscles cramped often. This night, she dreamed a giant turtle crawled up from the nearby stream and took a bite out of her leg. She woke with a cramp in her calf, and heard the muffled footsteps in the next room, where the Moder slept.

She heard the Moder's brief sharp cry, and the indescribable noise the cry became before it stopped. She thought the Moder must be dead. She hoped so; a person shouldn't have to live with whatever would make her sound like that.

Then three men came almost silently into the girls' dormitory, terribly quiet for men so large, one man to each child. She wondered, fleetingly, if there were three more men for the three boys next door. The men were dressed in black, with silver trim on their tunics and boots. Their heads – including their faces – were covered with black helmets, their hands with black gloves.

~*~

"Swords!" Kinnan rasped the word. "By the heart –" He strangled the rest of the sentence and clenched his hands together. "Go on, girl," he said, with grim quiet.

~*~

All this Tabby saw through nearly-closed eyes. Then her view was blocked by the man who stood next to her bed, by his hand filling her view, by the strong-smelling cloth in his hand. She was awake enough to gulp air before he caught her head in one hand and crushed his cloth against her face with the other.

Terrified, she went limp, and the man tied the ends of the cloth behind her head, making a poor job of it with trembling hands. She nearly cried out when the man stripped the shift from her body, but fear kept her silent. She felt the man lift her, carrying her through the Moder's room and into the night air. She managed to scrape the cloth against his arm, working it out of her mouth but not off her face.

The man dumped her into a barrel and closed the lid. She couldn't see. Her limbs felt heavy, her head felt stuffed, as if she had a cold and the Moder had given her medicine. She clawed the cloth away and fell into nightmare.

~*~

Kinnan covered his face with his hands. He breathed deeply, but a groan forced its way through his control. When he lowered his hands, his face was wet with tears. "This is not just a tale. Now I know why my sister left no heirs of the body. The child called Gosling was hers. If they killed the Moder, they killed the children, and took their bodies so no one would know what had happened to them."

"There are five baby farms in Layounna," Moder pointed out, "and more than one child in each one."

Kinnan's face twisted. "Not even Landry would…."

"He didn't know how many heirs there were," Moder said, "or where they were hidden. Had he given the task of finding them to his Chamberlain, the story would be kinder. But he turned another way, and it is as it is."

Kinnan rose, glaring at the door as if he would plunge into the night and run full-tilt to Kudasad to take immediate revenge. "By Tortoise, Unicorn, Phoenix and Dragon – by the four directions, by the elements, by all that lives and breathes and by all that doesn't – Landry has more to pay for than he has strength to endure!"

"But the child in this story, at least, escaped Landry's net," said Moder. "Sit, and listen."

Slowly, his body resisting the passive position, Kinnan sat.

Tabby didn't recognize the room in which she woke. The woman who sat on the edge of her bed was a stranger to her, and a man she didn't know stood nearby. She asked after the other children, about the farm and the cow and the chickens, and was told she'd dreamed them. She asked for the Moder, and the stranger-woman wept and said,

"I'm your mother, Elsie, dear. My name is Devona beren Valda. You are my only child, my precious treasure, and your name is Elsie beren Devona."

Kinnan turned a stricken look to Moder. She met his look, nodded, and returned her attention to the young woman who continued, still seeming to speak from a place deep within herself.

~*~

"My name isn't Elsie," Tabby whispered, trying to remember the face above her, the hand stroking her brow. "They call me Tabby."

"A pet name for babies," the stranger-man said harshly, then smiled as if he meant to be pleasant. When he spoke again, his voice was sweet. "Your name is Elsie." He went into another room and came back with something between his fingers. He held it up for her to see: it looked like a lump of glass the size of a dried bean, but angular, sides random and uneven.

"That isn't what she needs, Darcy," said the woman.

Darcy winked and said, "Open wide."

Tabby – Elsie – opened her mouth and Darcy put the lump on her tongue. It was sugar, flavored with peppermint! She smiled.

Darcy chuckled and patted her hand. "That's my girl," he said.

Kinnan stirred, a look of wary hope on his face. "Is it possible?" he asked Moder Zglaria. "Have I misjudged Landry? Elsie was placed with a foster family. Were they all?"

Elsie shook her head slowly, the spell of the story fading, her memory restored. "My mother – Devona told me …Darcy… was told to throw a wagon-load of barrels into the inland sea. When he finally opened one, he found Tabby. He found… me. I was the last one. The others…. Ellis, Garrick, Keenan, Agnes…Gosling…." Face raised, her hands loose on her lap, Elsie wept.

Kinnan re-settled into grimness. "Then I have a score to settle with this Darcy, as well."

"He didn't know." Elsie seemed surprised at her own protest. "He didn't know."

"His life hangs by your word. And so does Landry's." Kinnan leaned toward her. "Now will you come with me when I ride against the usurper? When you tell this tale, the people will roar for his blood!"

"Like savage animals," said Moder Zglaria. "Passion and compassion out of balance, mind and heart out of harmony. Do you remedy death with more of the same?"

"What should his reward be for what he's done? Should I give him the mandate myself?"

"No, indeed. The mandate is yours. You told me so."

Churning with rage – at Landry, at Darcy, at the old woman who refused to let anything be simple – Kinnan slammed out of the cottage and took refuge in his stall in the shed. There, he could lay schemes and plot revenge without confusion, though neither enterprise brought him the comfort he had expected.

Inside the cottage, the three women retired in silence. Elsie lay awake for a long time, gazing into the embers on the hearth, and wept for children no one but she remembered.

CHAPTER 16
THE SCRIVENER'S APPRENTICE

Neither Brady nor Sorcha slept after he returned from finding Hayward. Sorcha made him tell, in a whisper, all he knew of Karol and all he knew of Kinnan. She made him replay his conversation with her husband until he found it simpler to shift to Hayward's form and act it out.

The next morning, Mistress Brina came to see why Sorcha wasn't at her usual tasks. Sorcha pleaded headache and a sleepless night. That afternoon, saying she thought the fresh air would aid her recovery, Sorcha beren Moder kilted up her skirts and took her new dog for a walk. "She" returned late and alone, upset because the dog had run away. "She" retired to "her" rooms.

The next morning, when Waymistress Brina swept into the chambers full of the foolish rumor that Sorcha had taken refuge at Oakwood, "Sorcha" was gone.

Brady had opened the shutters of Sorcha's cell and slipped out as soon as the Waystation was quiet and dark. He thought it best to take an animal shape, just in case, but not another dog – he was sick of the wet hair smell. He'd have liked to be a newt, for the pleasure of sliding through the wet grass, but the middle of the night was not the safest time for newts, and he wouldn't travel very far very fast that way. He settled on an owl again, although he didn't much like damp feathers, either.

He was over the Kudasad Bridge when he realized he wasn't going anywhere until he'd seen Devona. How could he pass so close to her and not tell her of her daughter's safety? She might have given up by now; might begin and end her days with a curse for Brady birn Ilka, who wasn't to be trusted, in the end.

The Brady-owl banked and returned to the manor. A glow came from the ground-floor windows of the living quarters. Candles or rushes; not the strong light of crisis, but the grudging light of lingering contention.

Brady dropped to the ground and became a weasel, sniffing and prying along the foundation, stretching to his full height up the wall, searching for an entry. The only crack he could find was a small one on the shop side. Memory told him it was hidden inside by shelving. He put a paw in it, jumped, and shifted into a mouse. The mouse's hind feet scrabbled and scraped, found purchase on a splinter, and pushed.

He crouched just inside the hole, waiting for the mouse's tiny heart to calm, then crept around the walls to the inner door. Flattening himself, Brady slipped his mouse body under the door and dashed across the hall to the sitting room.

He tucked himself behind a carved oak chest and listened.

"Do you know more than you're telling me? If so, speak."

Brady recognized Darcy's voice, meant to sound masterful but coming out peevish in the face of his wife's composure.

"*I* wasn't with her when she disappeared," Devona said. "*You* were. I wasn't invited to the castle that day, remember? In fact, I had nothing to do with her coming *or* going, did I? Who put her into my arms in place of our own dead baby? Who had me bury my precious...." Devona's poise left her; her voice broke and she stopped speaking.

Brady's mouse ears pricked at this news. *Does Elsie know*?

Darcy said nothing to the charge and Devona went on at last, her voice rough with lack of weeping.

"How dare you question me – you, who've never given me your confidences?"

Brady could imagine her, small and plump and brown, her face raised defiantly to her husband's towering above her, her brown eyes flashing behind her round spectacles, her smooth chestnut hair coiled around her head in braids, perhaps with a quill or two stuck through a coil and forgotten.

"I've told you," Darcy said, "I've seen Elsie many times at the castle. Why do you say you know nothing of her? You feed the rumors of Elsie's ill-use or even –" Darcy laughed uncomfortably "–her vanishment."

"Well, hasn't she vanished? If she is in the castle, hasn't she left the face of the earth as surely as if she were spirited away, or as dead as our own Elsie?"

"Hush, woman!"

"Hush, yourself! I don't dance when you lift your hands. Look to your own strings, puppet!"

Brady heard an edge to his Mistress's voice he had never heard before. He rebuked himself for not having come to her sooner; she must be wild with worry. And here was Darcy, lying for the crown, even to her, and her knowing he lied, and unable to do more than seem to doubt. Brady decided to wait until Devona was alone and reveal himself to her. If his part in Elsie's escape were unsuspected, he could resume his own form: Devona's innocent clerk, back from a protracted business errand.

"Watch what you say, Devona. At times, you come perilously close to treason."

Devona made a scornful sound. "I haven't your taste for politics. Treason doesn't interest me."

"That's my dear wife." Darcy's voice was breathy and over-bright with relief. "Well, let's speak no more of it tonight. We've been together so long, I forget your origins. It's in your blood, to want evidence you can see and touch; you distrust what you have to imagine."

Darcy's patronizing tone set Brady's teeth on edge. He had to gnaw at the chest that sheltered him to take away the itch. It helped, knowing that the chest was a particular prize of Darcy's, a relic of his merchant family.

Brady hoped that Darcy would leave Devona alone after that, but it was Devona who left the room, kicking the hem of her skirt before her.

Darcy heaved a deep sigh when her candle's light had faded up the stairs.

"No," Darcy said, and Brady peeked from behind the chest to see if there were another person in the room. There wasn't. Darcy stood alone near the center of the chamber, long and slim and hard-looking as a birch rod. A thin braid behind either ear held his lank white-gold hair away from his creamy face. A drooping mustache framed his tight-lipped mouth.

Darcy rubbed his face with one fine hand and pinched the bridge of his nose. "Nothing to fear."

Even as Darcy said this, pain stabbed Brady's back. A soft weight, like a feather-bed studded with needles, pressed him to the floor.

He felt a blast of hot air from above and a deep vibration through the pain. Elsie's tortoiseshell cat, Trenel, had him. The tortoiseshell dropped from the chest to the floor beside it. Brady rolled limply, as Trenel scooped him out.

"What is it?" said Darcy. "A mouse? Well, you're good for something, after all."

Brady squeaked. Trenel softly squashed him again.

"This was a bad house to come to, pest," said Darcy. "We have protection against your kind. Now, you get what you deserve for nibbling what others have earned and fouling what others have stored. Play with it, Trenel, but don't let it get away."

Darcy settled back to watch the sport.

Trenel's teeth were terribly close; his breath came out in bursts of savage purrs.

It would be so easy, Brady thought, to turn to a dog and give his captor a lasting shock. That would mean giving up a secret to Darcy, though, and that was a last resort.

The cat lay down and curled his paws around his victim, as if cuddling him. He stuck his nose into the embrace and sniffed.

"Don't – please don't!" Brady thought, assuming that his squeals and chitterings were the mouse-shape's translation. "I'm not a mouse, I'm Brady! You know me!"

Trenel froze. He growled, clashed his teeth within a whisker's width of Brady, and pulled back. He crouched, tail lashing. Then he leapt, turned in mid-air, streaked across the room, and bit Darcy through the ankle of his soft house-boots.

Darcy yelped and threw his leg into the air, then stomped back down and kicked at the cat with his other foot. Trenel sprang out of his reach, sauntered back to the Brady-mouse, and sat on him, eyes slitted in satisfaction.

Devona brought her candle half-way down the stairs. "What is it? What's happened?"

"This cursed cat of Elsie's bit me!"

"Did you try to pet him?"

"No! I should hope I know better than that! I was watching him play with a mouse and he ran over and bit me!"

"He was just over-excited, poor thing." Devona, sounded, from her tone, as if she hoped Trenel had gotten in a good one, while he was at it.

"Poor thing? Poor cat, poor mouse, poor everybody but me!"

"Well, come here and let's look at the wound. I'll clean it and put a poultice on it and bind it up. Poor Darcy." The term sounded weary, and full of pity and resignation.

Brady lay, paralyzed by the mouse body's terror, as Devona led Darcy to the kitchen and treated his "wound." He lay still as the couple went up the stairs together, said a warmer goodnight than they had for many years, and shut themselves into their separate rooms.

Trenel stood up but, when one of the doors opened again, he resumed his seat.

Light and footsteps came down the stairs and into the room – Devona hadn't forgotten the mouse, after all.

"Where is it? Poor beast – if it's alive, I'll put it out. Where is it? Are you sitting on it?"

She tried to push the cat off his prey with a stick of kindling, but Trenel made himself as heavy as any cat who doesn't want to move.

At last, in the warmth of the cat's body, the mouse's shock reaction faded, and Brady stirred.

"You will get up, Master Trenel." Devona gasped as the mouse became Brady, lying on his back with a placid cat balanced on his stomach.

"My back!" Brady groaned. "He stabbed me!"

Trenel yawned.

"And he's squashing my belly. The *weight* of this beast!" Brady rolled the cat off onto the floor.

Devona held up a silencing hand. She padded into the hall, looked up to make certain Darcy's door was shut, and came back. "Are you hurt badly?"

"A little more than pinpricks, I think, but only a little more. He saved his worst for Master Darcy. – Do you know, I believe he knew me, once he'd caught me. I think he bit the Master because his blood was up, and he didn't want to kill his old friend Brady, not even as a mouse." He reached and rubbed Trenel's face. "Is that it? Eh?"

Trenel was fast, but Brady was faster, and the cat's teeth clacked together with nothing but air between them.

"Nasty brute," Brady muttered.

"Where have you been?" Devona's glasses shone blankly in the candle-light. "Where is Elsie?"

"She's safe. She's not in Kozabir, but she's safe."

Devona crouched by Brady and took his shoulders in hands made strong by fear. "What do you mean? Why isn't she in Kozabir?" She shook her apprentice roughly. "Where is my daughter?"

"She's safe! You're hurting me, Mistress! Be calm, I'll tell you."

Devona let the boy go, and laid her trembling hands across her knees.

"She's in the Fiddlewood with an old woman."

"An old woman in the Fiddlewood.... Near Pazni?"

"You know her?"

"I know of her. Darcy was full of her when he took office; how he was going to see her for himself, that she'd been on the rolls so long he doubted she existed."

"Oh, she exists."

"He found that out. He came back quietly and never spoke of her again. Until Landry chose Elsie, of all the women in Layounna. Then Darcy packed his saddlebags and rode off. He said it was to make a surprise audit of the Pazni records, but he acted strangely. Then he.... Something he said told me where he'd been and who he'd seen." Devona looked away from Brady, remembering her husband gripped with respect for something outside his own self-interest. "She's safe with the old woman."

Trenel yowled. Brady and Devona both jumped. In the upper hall, a board creaked.

Devona peered out of the room. Darcy stood near the top of the dark staircase, leaning over the rail.

"Who's there?" he demanded.

"Only me."

"I heard voices. More than one."

"I'm alone."

"Do you speak out loud when you're alone?"

"Sometimes."

"Someone's with you."

"Only Trenel. I threw his mouse in the fire. I've been explaining. I know he doesn't understand—"

Darcy came down the stairs. "Who's with you?" There was fear in Darcy's voice, fear trying to disguise itself as intelligent caution.

Devona looked desperately over her shoulder at Brady. As Darcy's tread sounded in the hall, Devona scooped Trenel off the floor and dumped him out of the casement in a practiced sweep. Brady disappeared, and another Trenel sat before the fire.

Darcy stepped into the room and looked around. Chair, chair, bench, small table; all standing high on straight, carved legs; carved chest, too close to the wall to hide anything larger than a mouse.

"Are you satisfied? Who did you think you'd find?"

"What's that noise outside?"

"A friend of Trenel's, I suppose, asking him if he can come out."

"He sounds like he's cursing."

"If you're content that I'm alone…."

"Where is that apprentice of yours? Is he never coming back?" Darcy, wary eyes fixed on the cat, didn't see his wife's mouth pop open at this unexpected sally.

"Is that who you thought was here?"

"I was sure I heard two voices. Who else would you admit at this hour and not call me? Assuming you told the truth when you said treason doesn't interest you."

"Well, aren't you clever, to puzzle all that out? Brady is the only person who could be here, but you see he isn't. Perhaps he's left us for good."

"Taking your money along. I never liked that boy. I never trusted him."

"Trenel" growled and laid his ears back.

Darcy went to the fireplace and stirred up the remains of the logs. "I thought you said you threw the mouse in here."

"Did you want it?"

The Roll-Keeper gave his wife an irritated glance. "No, I don't want it. I just don't see it."

"Perhaps it–" Devona began, but Darcy turned away from her and sat on the fireside bench, taking the poker with him.

"If that cat looks like biting me again–" he pointed at "Trenel" with the poker, "–I'll brain it."

"He won't bite you." Devona stifled a laugh at the disgusted look Brady managed to put on the cat's face.

Darcy sighed and patted the bench by his side, an old and long-unused invitation to Devona to be near him.

She sat next to her husband. Most of Darcy's length was in his legs and little of Devona's was; seated, they were close to the same height. She slid an arm around his shoulders, feeling as if she had slipped into the past, or into a dream. It seemed another world or another life, the time when she and Darcy had shared any softness with each other. Two moments in one evening – it was almost unbearably dear.

"On the other hand, who could blame the boy for bolting?" Darcy's voice vibrated along Devona's arm. "Layounna is on the brink of ruin. No doubt he deserted us before we sank. Vermin like that have an instinct for saving their own skins, I'm told."

"'Vermin' like what?" Devona's voice was icy, her arm suddenly stiff and heavy. "Apprentices? Have you forgotten I came to your family as an apprentice? Or have you not?"

Darcy looked into his wife's face. "I didn't mean you." He stared at her for several long moments. She stared back, grimly.

When he spoke again, it was as if the years had rolled away like so many stones. "The things I've done," he said softly. "The things I've done."

"What things?" Devona whispered.

And Darcy told her. She let him tell it, resisting the impulse to spare herself by telling him she'd heard it before.

Brady sat shivering on the hearth, listening.

"When Landry chose Elsie as his bride," Darcy said, "I was afraid. For us and for Elsie." He looked away. "Mostly for myself," he said quietly. "Then she disappeared, and now…."

"What is it?"

"As you say, you were never very political, but even you must sense rebellion in the air. Something will happen, and soon. I was given this promotion and transfer because of my service to Landry that night. Yet I betrayed the trust he put in me; I saved one child. And she's gone – how? where?"

"I don't understand what you're saying."

Darcy shook his head. "I hardly know myself. – The power of Sarpa is eroding. Can it shore itself up? Will Landry use what I've done for him against me to his own advantage? If Sarpa falls, will we fall, too?"

Forgetful of the cat-shaped audience on the hearth, Devona wound her arms around her husband's neck as she had not done since the death of their true daughter a decade before. Darcy dropped the poker. He held her tightly, still frightened, but clinging to a certainty he'd lost over the years: Devona.

"Perhaps things aren't quite that desperate yet," said Darcy. "But I think…I really think that Sarpa cannot stand."

No doubt you'll desert it before it sinks, Master, Brady thought. *Vermin have an instinct for saving their own skins, I'm told.*

Neither Darcy nor Devona noticed when "Trenel" left the room. No one saw a mouse leave through a hole in the storeroom wall, and no one saw an owl rise above the manor and fly through the mist and drizzle toward Fiddlewood to the north.

chapter 17
GRANOMOOER'S GIFT

Nerissa, blazingly awake after her day's nap, waited until she was certain, doubly certain, Tartarus was asleep. Then she rose and eased out of the door, shutting it behind her. She crept farther along the shelf before climbing up to the moor. A mist, opalescent in the moonlight, rose from the sea. The vapor thickened and rolled in and up the bluff, surrounding her, blinding her. Then she saw, from its heart, two eyes staring at her.

They were dark, though they were visible when nothing else was, and wider and deeper than a human's. They came closer and Nerissa saw a large face that glowed faintly, lighting the mist nearby with blue-green radiance. Its muzzle was long and rounded, its mouth opened to show two rows of sharp white teeth.

The thing slid onto the heath, first its head, then its neck, then two clawed legs, then a long body, then two more clawed legs, then a tail. It was covered with scales, and its breath was soft and warm.

Nerissa had seen dragons on some of the Emir's banners – terrible and beautiful. Her hair stood on end, but she felt no impulse to scream or run, only the impulse to look, and look, and wait.

"Don't be afraid, Little Pigeon," said the dragon. "I wouldn't hurt you for the world. I am Verrina beren Unna. But you may call me Grandmoder."

The girl put out a hesitant hand and touched the dragon's scales. They were soft, like feathers. "Are you *my* grandmother?"

"No, but I'm somebody's, and that will do."

"I never had a grandmother of my own."

"Of course you did, my dove. You never met her, that's all. But everybody has one. More than one, in fact." The dragon laughed, a burbly hissing laugh, like a kettle just on the boil.

"Am I…? Am I really the sea king's daughter? Is that why you're here? To take me back into the sea?"

"No to both questions, dear child. I've come to steal you away from Tartarus. *I* never promised *I* wouldn't. Tartarus is clever, but I know a trick worth two of his." The monster's eyes gleamed tenderly. "Climb on my back, if you're willing."

Was that the promise Tartarus had dared Farukh to break? Farukh had wanted to take her away, but Tartarus had already made him promise he wouldn't! Her friend had wanted to take her with him! The joy of that knowledge burned away the last of her hurt and disappointment. Even her anger at Tartarus turned into a pleasure, now that she had an ally in thwarting him.

With a shiver of delight, she climbed on the dragon's back. How could she refuse this invitation from wonder?

The scaled creature slipped through the air like a calm river between its banks, and the wind of its passage was gentle. Nerissa caught glimpses of the water below through open patches in the mist. Now there would be a sea between her and Granitz, between her and Tartarus. Good.

By and by, they came to the other shore and the dragon landed.

"This is the northern edge of the Geiskeflor. Here I leave you."

"The Geiskeflor!" Tales of the Haunted Wood were common in Granitz. It was said that even Tortoise was wary of it. Nerissa threw her arms around the dragon's neck. "Don't leave me! I'm afraid!"

"Afraid? A girl who's looked Tartarus in the eye and not backed down? Now, then, my duck, there's nothing to be afraid of. I don't abandon you. I leave you with a companion, a remembrance, and a word of instruction. The companion is that." The dragon lifted her snout toward the moon. "The gift is this." The dragon wept one tiny tear, which rolled off her feathery cheek to fall into the child's open hand as a tiny, perfect pearl. "The instruction: Some day, perhaps quite soon, you will be walking along a path in another country."

"Another country?"

The dragon nodded. "There, you'll see an old man with no hair, pulling a cart. Say nothing to him, but do as he says. Repeat that, child."

"An old man with no hair, pulling a cart; I say nothing to him, but do as he says."

"Obey me, and all will be well in the end."

And then, too quickly to be held or mourned, the dragon was gone.

Nerissa looked up at the moon, to find that clouds covered the sky, and the light that bathed her shone from her bird, perched on a nearby tree.

A dismal fog descended, a fine mist that penetrated her rags.

Nerissa once more followed the bright bird who flitted before her and shone through the damp like a chalk rainbow just before it washes away. After they had gone some distance, the bird dissolved and vanished. Nerissa stood, unbelieving, frozen in faith, waiting for her guide to reappear.

When it didn't, she sighed deeply and sat down to rest her weary legs.

For the first time since she had run away, she gave real thought to what was to become of her. She had heard that, beyond the Geiskeflor, there was another entire country, every bit as big as Kozabir. The country Grandmoder had prophesied for her? She would go there and learn the language, sure to be one of the strange tongues she had heard spoken in Granitz. She didn't expect much, though she hoped for better than she'd had. Her rosiest dream was of enough bread nearly every night and thread to repair her ragged dress. She still had the pennies she'd saved in Granitz. They would keep her from starving until she could earn more. She would find work somewhere – she was a hard worker. Even Tartarus would have to admit….

She shivered with cold and solitude, but felt a touch of comfort in the contemplation of Tartarus's fury when he found she had given him the slip. The bleak possibility that he wouldn't care shriveled under the memory of his badgering. He would miss picking at her, if nothing else.

Now, even Tartarus would have been a friendly presence. Farukh was gone, Grandmoder was gone, the moon was invisible, and the wonderful bird had faded away. It would come back – of that, Nerissa was certain, but it was gone now, and she had never felt so alone.

She was hungry, but that was so far from unusual she didn't notice it. What she did notice was how cold the fog had become. She thrust her bony hands into the pockets of her skirt.

Her right hand touched warmth and curled around it.

Grandmoder's pearl. The heat spread, warming and drying her as if by a soft and arid breath. Her treasure – the only gift she had ever been given.

Then her pocket began to glow, as if the cloth were hung before a fire. She withdrew her hand, still wrapped around the pearl. Her hand shone, a mild gray-brown light. Slowly, breath held and eyes unblinking, Nerissa uncurled her fingers and let the pearl shine unblocked. It cast a radiance that didn't dazzle, but lit a space three arms-lengths around. It lay cupped in her palm, a little larger than a grain of barley, and shone with the silver-white intensity of a full moon.

By the pearl's glow, she saw a path. Slowly, carefully, she stood. She held her hand low, and took a step. The light seemed brighter to the left. She turned that way, and so did the path. She could almost hear the undergrowth pull aside for her as she walked, then rustle closed behind her.

The Geiskeflor was completely silent. It was as if the fog or the pearl or something else held her apart from the world around her.

She didn't know how long she had been walking when the pearl's light led her to a pile of smooth stones as high as her head.

The stones shifted silently.

Nerissa grasped the dragon's pearl as she started backward in alarm. The stones were alive! Nerissa opened her hand again; she would rather see this thing than have it there, moving unseen.

As her eyes adjusted from seeing a pile of rocks to seeing a living animal, its form clarified. It was some sort of horse, she thought – larger than the ceremonial mounts used in the Emir's parades, bred to carry giants in armor. It lay on the ground, its legs folded under it… and it had only one foreleg, placed in the center of its chest. It was the color of a heavy winter day, when the whole sky is cloud. Nerissa's eyes widened as her gaze traveled up the creature's neck, past a thick and heavy mane of darker gray, to the massive head, to the horn striped in two shades of half-light.

Nerissa had heard of Unicorn, but she had never heard it described. She had a rather vague mental picture of one, something like a shaggy goat with one of its horns broken off. She certainly would have made no connection between that foolish, unkempt image and this magnificent monster, but she knew instantly what this was.

"Unicorn?" Nerissa didn't expect a reply, but she wasn't surprised to hear the voiceless answer.

I'm a story that shrinks in the telling. It extended its muzzle toward her, then stopped when she jerked as if to run. *And you are called Nerissa.*

Whisper: "How do you know me?"

I know you. "How" is a long story, and leads a different way. It pleases me to see you.

Nerissa took a step nearer. There was power in the unicorn, as there was light in Grandmoder's pearl even when it was wrapped in cloth and flesh. The power reached out to her and drew her, but she sensed the power was faded. "You're hurt?"

No, child. But I will be. The huge head lowered and turned, jaw and horn-tip resting on the ground. The eyes closed, and the world grew darker.

A dozen very small steps, and Nerissa was at the creature's side. She knelt and put a hesitating hand up against the unicorn's ribs. She wanted to feel it breathe. She wanted to feel its heart beat. She needed to know it was alive. "What can I do?"

Nothing, child. I only wanted to see you pass. I never meant for you to see me.

"But I did. This showed you to me."

The unicorn raised its head and opened both its eyes. *A dragon's pearl?*

Nerissa's hand wavered as she struggled to leave her treasure extended and exposed. "Yes. She said it was a gift."

Light, health, and strength. A precious gift. May it serve you well. Its head sank to the ground again, its eyes closed once more.

"Don't die! Please don't die!" Nerissa felt tears pour from her as if she had never wept before.

I'm not dying. I'm only weak. At any rate, it doesn't matter.

"It does matter! It matters to me!" Impossible to have found such beauty in the world, and watch it die! She rolled the pearl to her fingertips and grasped it in a pinch. She leaned far forward and slipped a hand under the unicorn's muzzle.

The eyes opened slowly. *I'm not dying,* the unicorn repeated. *Keep your treasure.*

"This is what it's for." She thrust the pearl between the unicorn's soft lips and was left in nearly total darkness. The weight of the huge head lifted. With her right hand, Nerissa touched the wall of flesh beside her and felt it ripple with new strength.

You're a wise little owl, she heard the unicorn say, and then it was gone.

Once again, the girl was alone in the dark. But there...to her right, through the trees, she saw a glimmer of light. As she peered at it, it grew and spread, as if it were water pouring from a fountain. The light gushed and streamed, changing course to curve around trees and rocks, until it seemed to fall into the earth before her.

It had been a night of marvels, but Nerissa never wondered if she might be dreaming. She had never felt so wide-awake. She rose and stepped onto the surface of the liquid light. It was warm, and warmed her from toe to top. Step by step, she followed the light to its source: an ordinary tin lantern on the porch of a wooden house. Only when she reached it did she look behind her; she saw nothing but misty darkness.

There were no lights burning inside the house, but she knew she was welcome. She carried the lantern in with her, and found a pot of fresh hot stew on the hearth. She ate, washed, curled up on the floor, and went to sleep.

~*~

Nerissa dreamed she was struggling to wake. Her mind and spirit felt oppressed, her body paralyzed, though her heart strained with effort. When she did wake she lay, groggy and exhausted, on the floor. It was barely morning. A gray-green light cast dappled shadows-against-shadows all around her.

She sensed movement nearby. Tortoise – a tortoise a yard long, creeping, about to bite!

She cried out and drew herself up. Then the "tortoise" raised its head and *miaouw*ed, and she recognized the tortoiseshell cat from Tartarus's hut.

"Oh! How did you get here?" *Tartarus – here?* No, if Tartarus had come after her, it was hardly likely he would have shared his coracle with the cat. Besides that, she felt sure her old Master would have wakened her with a roar, possibly with a shaking. She looked at the door and saw it was still firmly shut and bolted. "How did you get in?" She put out a hand and stroked the head that ducked away too slowly to avoid the touch. "You're soaked! Poor thing." Before the cat could run or claw, Nerissa picked him up and wrapped him in her skirt. "Now you'll get dry and warm."

The cat growled savagely, all muscles tense as if wound to their most explosive tightness.

"Now, don't do that. I'm not hurting you. It doesn't hurt you a bit to be loved. I missed you." She rubbed the cat's head, the only part of him that showed. The cat made a half-hearted snap at her fingers, then seemed to sigh and give up. He relaxed, a silly, careless look on his face, and even ventured a rusty purr.

"The unicorn is gone," Nerissa told him. "But that doesn't mean it's safe. It said it was going to be hurt. It looked so sad. So tired and weak. It said it didn't matter if it died. But you should have seen it."

The cat suddenly flipped himself out of Nerissa's arms. He danced out of range and shook himself, one foot at a time. His hair stood up in spikes all over his head and body.

"What's the matter?"

The cat looked over his shoulder at her and yowled.

"Are *you* hurt? Come here and let me see."

The cat slid into the shadows. Nerissa scrambled after him, then heard his yowl outside.

How did he do that? She opened the door. "How did you do that?"

He quick-footed into the woods and Nerissa ran after him.

All day they traveled, due east, dodging and darting on and off the path. Whenever Nerissa stopped to rest, her cat prowled around as if on guard, and growled and muttered until she stood and followed him again. When the girl was too weary and hungry to move another step, the cat found a bush of those lovely blue-black berries from the heath above Tartarus's cliff; she ate her fill and, refreshed, continued.

Darkness came quickly under the forest canopy.

"Oh, cat!" Nerissa said. "I can't see you and I can't see the path. I know you're leading me somewhere, although Grandmoder never mentioned you…." Briefly, this troubled the child but, in truth, she felt more kinship with the shabby cat than she did with the glorious dragon. "I'm going to stop here for the night. Right here."

She stretched out where she was. She thought she had her eyes open, hoping the cat would come and curl up with her, but she must have fallen asleep and dreamed.

Three patches of white shimmered into being, then became the face and hands of an old woman dressed in black. The old woman thumped the ground with the blackthorn stick she used as a cane, and the cat slunk out of the woods and sat between her and Nerissa.

"She's mine," he said, in Tartarus's voice. "Farukh promised to leave her to me."

"Farukh is not what he once was, as you well know."

The cat gave an ugly chuckle.

The old woman stood passively. She and the cat seemed to be waiting something out. After a while, the cat raised his left hind leg and washed it, beginning at his toes. The old woman watched, saying nothing.

Eventually, he stopped and said, "Do you have no shame? Look away, won't you?"

"Take my eyes off you? I don't think I care to. Anything you're not too proud to do, I'm not too proud to look at."

"She's mine," he repeated.

"Why don't we try her and see? You've had your chance with her. Are you afraid you're losing your touch? Afraid the tarnish might wear off?"

"I didn't have much to do, with this one. She grew up in the gutter to begin with. Nasty temper. Underhanded. Ill-natured. Not much for me to spoil."

"Then there's nothing to worry about."

"I'm not worried. But you can't have her."

The old woman nodded slowly, sadly. "All right, I can't have her. At least let me carry her for you."

The cat's voice was suspicious. "Carry her where?"

"Into the heart of corruption. Into the very heart, your very stronghold, where blood is shed for you daily."

"You would do that? You would take her there?"

"I would."

The cat seemed to be considering this. Then he turned to Nerissa, who narrowed her eyes and watched him through the slits. *Let me go, let me go. Grandmoder would want it – I can feel it. Let me go.*

"Guttersnipe," he said. "Take her, then."

Nerissa had an *almost* uncontrollable urge to grab the cat and press him to her heart. He had released her from something, released her *to* something.

Her eyes closed all the way, then, and she eased into deep sleep.

She woke to a clear night and a fresh breeze. The ground below her was moving! She clutched the earth, to find it warm and alive. Smooth skin over heavy muscle, and hair – no, a mane. Was she on a horse? No. Without seeing, she knew she was stretched out on the back of the unicorn.

We've crossed the River, it said.

"Where are you taking me?"

Farther along the way you would have taken on your own.

The unicorn stepped from beneath the forest canopy, into the starlight. *Now sit straight, hold the ends of my mane, not the roots, and don't be frightened. I won't let you fall.*

Three strides, and the unicorn was galloping, if that was the proper term for its three-legged gait. Nerissa could feel the bunch and stretch of muscle between her bare heels as the central front leg pushed and reached and bit and pushed again.

Whatever they passed, they passed in a blur. The wind played in Nerissa's hair and patted at her face, yet surely the unicorn's speed should have knocked her off her perch. Nor was there any sound from hooves that should have broken the rocks as they struck.

Nerissa didn't care. She was living a story, better than any overheard bits of Farukh's, better than any she'd invented for herself, even better than the two Farukh had told for her alone. What was happening was what ought to happen, and she didn't question it.

Too soon, the ride was over. The unicorn stood still, darker in the first glimmerings of dawn than it had been in the night.

They stood in a copse near the river. Through gaps in branches, Nerissa could see parts of a bridge.

Kudasad Bridge, the unicorn said. *Cross it. See what happens. Are you frightened?*

"No." Nerissa slid to the ground. "I'm free, and protected by magic."

Child, you are not.

Nerissa looked up into the massive face.

You must protect yourself, the unicorn said, *by being careful and clever. Do nothing until you're sure of what you do and never hesitate once you're sure. Nothing else protects you.*

The child looked at Kudasad Bridge and moved closer to the beast.

I can give you a gift, the unicorn said, *in exchange for the one you gave up for me.* It lowered its muzzle to Nerissa's ear. Nerissa's hair stirred with the creature's breath. *A gift of language. You can speak and under-stand the language of Layounna. Layounna is this country's name, and Kudasad is its capital. Across that bridge and at the end of that road.*

"Is that where I'm going?"

To the castle.

The castle! How often she had longed for a place in the Emir's pal-ace! How she had envied those servants, with clean water to drink and to wash in – and food every day, she had heard.

"Thank you!"

It's too early to know if I deserve your thanks or your curse. They worship Tortoise in the castle – the Lady of the castle does, at least. She offers bloody sacrifices to him.

Nerissa shuddered. Then she remembered the second story Farukh had told in Tartarus' hut. "I'll keep out of the lady's way. I'm not afraid of Tortoise. She might belong to him, but he doesn't belong to her."

Brave words. The deeds are up to you. It turned away from the – the new words came to Nerissa, surprising and savory, like an unexpected taste – the Fiddlewood River.

"No, wait!" Nerissa clasped strands of mane. "I know you can't stay, but – will I see you again?"

Not in your hour of desperation. After that, perhaps. With a shake, it freed its mane and stepped into the river. It shoved off the bank and swam north, back the way it had come, leaving Nerissa alone again. She watched the unicorn until its silent, foaming wake was out of sight, then picked her way through the brush to the Eastern Road.

She heard hoofbeats and spring-creaks before she reached the edge of the trees. Wagons drawn by donkeys and horses, carts drawn by goats and people, men and women and children carrying baskets on their shoulders or backs or heads converged on the road, most of them turning toward the capital and, Nerissa assumed, the market there.

She walked alone, her fears quieted by the murmur of voices muted by dawn. She listened closely to the alien cadences and vowels, and was delighted to understand what scraps of conversation she could hear.

The bridge was an adventure; Nerissa had never seen a bridge so large, nor a river as strong and swift as Fiddlewood. It was one thing to cross such a current on the back of a fabulous beast, another to cross on a structure of wood laid end-to-end and side-by-side. Still, no one else seemed to think anything of it, so Nerissa hesitated only a moment. She glanced once over the railing, but the rushing water made her giddy, and she looked ahead after that. She was glad to be on solid ground again, part of the thickening crowd, weaving in and out among the walkers and vehicles.

A plaza opened before her, rimmed with booths and vendors' carts. The crowded road reminded her of Granitz, and the memory made her uneasy. She hurried on, not even stopping to watch a puppet show that was just beginning.

With the suddenness of a closing door, the rumble and mutter ended and Nerissa walked alone. There was no sound. Around a bend in the road appeared a roil of mist. Out of that mist walked an old man. He was dressed in a coarse brown tunic, and wore leather boots. He was bald, and pulled a cart, as many of Nerissa's fellow-travelers had done, though this man pulled his load as if it were weightless. The only sounds Nerissa heard were the turn of the cart's wheels and the regular clump of the man's booted feet on the dusty road.

"Good day, child," he called.

Some day, perhaps quite soon, you will be walking along a path in another country. There, you'll see an old man with no hair, pulling a cart. Say nothing to him, but do as he says.

Nerissa stepped off the road, away from the man. She lifted her near shoulder, half afraid of him. *You must protect yourself by being careful and clever. Nothing else protects you.*

"I dropped a razor in the ditch this side of the road," the man said. "Two turns back. Find it, and put it in your pocket. Ask for Biddi. Tell her the hen lays well."

Nerissa sidled past, just off the road, feeling her way with her bare feet, unable to take her eyes off the man and his cart. She could see what he was pulling, now: a very small jumble of things, including a black kettle and a black-and-white hen.

"She must think I'm mad," the man said.

Nerissa walked more quickly.

"Two turns back, mind," the old man called. "And ask for Biddi."

Nerissa rounded the bend, expecting to walk into the mist from which the old man had emerged. There was no mist. She hurried on, eager now for ordinary company. Around a second bend, the road became populated once more, with crowds behind and around her as well as ahead.

The grass was thick, and the old man's directions had been vague. She hoped for another wonder, for the metal to glint through the sheltering grass or for the grass to part for her. Nothing wonderful happened.

Nerissa knelt and peered into the ditch. It was dark under the over-hanging verge, and wet and dirty. She would never see a razor – she would have to feel for it. She hoped it was the kind they used in the marketplace of Granitz, the kind that folded away into its own handle. She must be careful not to be cut.

It took her the better part of an hour, sloshing in the muddy water, but she found it. It was a beautiful thing. The wet seemed to have done it no harm; it opened easily, liquid clay sliding from its surface like dreams from a waking mind. Its blued steel blade was carved with connected lines she thought might be letters that schooled folk could read. The handle/case was silver steel, etched with the stem and tiny flowers of a plant Nerissa didn't know. Carefully, she folded it shut and dropped it into her pocket.

"Biddi...." she said, and rejoined the throng heading for Kudasad.

Nerissa spent most of the day just outside the castle gate watching braver souls pass in and out. Finally, a woman in worn clothing and with a basket over her arm noticed her and stopped. The woman was nearly as brown as a Kozabiri, with darker freckles arching across her nose. Her hair was a faded red with strands of yellowish-white. Her eyes were a pale clear blue.

"If you're begging, you'll have to do better than that," the woman said. She glanced toward the castle, as if she were waited for and lingered at some risk. It was a look Nerissa knew well.

"No, Lady – Yes, Lady – I know how to beg. I'm not begging."

"Looking for someone, then?"

Nerissa had been told to go to the castle, and she had been told to ask for Biddi. What she hadn't been told was whether she should ask for Biddi at the castle or in the castle or should have asked for her long before now.

"Are you hungry?" the woman asked.

Nerissa shook her head, but her stomach growled. She covered her mouth with a filthy hand and giggled.

The woman laughed, too. "That answers my question. Come with me. I'll find you a bite, and maybe you'll tell me who you want. Come on."

Nerissa walked very close to the woman as they passed between the Swords guarding the gate. She remembered the men in black and silver surrounding the tavern in Granitz that night so long ago. She still remembered the moonlight on their blades and the terror she'd felt for her friend the storyteller, somewhere in that tavern.

There were more Swords inside the castle but her companion passed them, nose in air, as if they were bugs on a wall.

To Nerissa's horror, the woman didn't stop inside the lower palisade, but went up the boardwalk of the earthen motte into the upper enclosure, where the tower stood, as big around as the Central Square in Granitz and four stories high, including the ground level. The girl lagged behind, staring with mouth agape and eyes wide. The castle tower! Where the Emir – Nerissa corrected herself in her new tongue – where the Kinninger lived! Villeins passed to and fro, carrying baskets, pulling carts, rolling barrels. A small smithy, new-built, was stuck to the side of the tower, giving the little workshop a temporary air.

Her guide was gone! With relief, Nerissa saw her new friend bustle back around the corner.

The woman smiled when she saw Nerissa, and shook her head as she came up to her. "I thought I'd lost you. Come around to the kitchen."

Nerissa followed around the corner and down a half-flight of stairs. The kitchen was warm and steamy and smelled of roasted beef and boiled vegetables. It was big, bigger than any of the wealthy kitchens of Granitz where Nerissa had waited for errands to run. There were two huge fire-places; one was empty now, but the other held a simmering cauldron. Nerissa could see a metal strip laid across the top, a thick string tied from the strip and hanging heavily into the pot. She sniffed. *Pudding*, she thought. Kitchen servants clustered around a large table at the other end of the room, grinding herbs and spices in stone mortars, chopping vegetables, filleting fish, cutting crusty oval loaves of bread in half and scooping out the crumbs inside, dumping the crumbs into a rectangular pan. Through an archway, Nerissa could see more activity in the room beyond.

Biddi stopped at a table just below the steps. Nerissa stood near her, taking all in with wide eyes and watering mouth.

A large, florid woman, her grizzled hair pulled back from her face, dominated the center of the room, directing the activities. She turned, pointed a spoon at Nerissa and said, "What's that?"

"I found her at the gate. She may want work. She needs a bite to eat."

"Hmmm. Well, there's plenty of waste at Their table. Wash her face and hands, if she's going to sit in the kitchen." She walked away abruptly.

Nerissa's new friend ladled some water into a basin and, with three changes of water, cleaned the worst of the grime. She gestured her to a corner stool as the large woman came back, holding one of the half-loaves, its hollow filled with food. "There's some vegetable cuttings and a bone I took out of the roast before I sent it in – plenty of meat on it."

Nerissa stood up. The woman shoved the bread at her.

"Well, take it!"

Nerissa took it, bewildered.

"Sit down! Eat!"

Nerissa thanked the women with her new words, and Grandmoder and the unicorn in the silence of her heart. This was the Safe Haven in the world – who could have dreamed such "scraps" as this?

"Did you bring those grapes?" the florid woman asked. "Good. SHE must have them, and have them tonight, never mind the trouble it gives. One thing I will say for you, Biddi – you've always been a willing worker. You could be taking my place when I go, instead of being a kitchen maid, and at your age, but…."

Nerissa heard no more of the cook's speech. Biddi! This was Biddi – this woman who had stopped for her, alone of all the crowd. She must give her the message she'd been ordered to deliver – but she wanted her alone when she did.

Biddi went about her work, smiling at Nerissa whenever she passed or looked up and caught her eye. Everyone else seemed to be ignoring the child, but at length there was a lull and the large woman, wiping her hands on a cloth, stood before her, looming like the castle tower itself.

"I'm Janet beren Lana. I'm the Head Cook, as you may have guessed. Now, what can you do, young one? – Besides eat."

Nerissa wiped her mouth on the backs of her hands and her hands on her ragged gown. "I can do a lot of things. I could go into town and bring back grapes."

The cook laughed. "You hear that, Biddi? The kitchen maid's assistant!"

"I can clean anything. I can lift heavy things. I can remember messages. I can learn."

The cook raised her eyebrows. "You're worth your weight in salt, if you can do that! What's your name, then?"

"Nerissa. Nerissa b-beren M-Moder."

"Where do you come from?"

"From… outside the city."

"Runaway?"

Terrified, Nerissa could only stare.

"I'm asking if somebody's liable to come looking for you, making trouble for me?"

Nerissa shook her head. Even supposing Barand Tara birn Isa should follow and find her, he'd crumble before Janet.

"Well, if Biddi wants you, Biddi can have you. You'll work under me, but pester her. Be within call if I need you, and stay out of my way when I don't. I've a short temper and a hard hand, and I tolerate no impertinence. Eh, Biddi?"

Biddi nodded, unsmiling.

~*~

At the end of her first day's work, Nerissa was strained and weary. The work was simple and easily done, but she was used to much more freedom of movement. Staying close yet out of the way had proved more difficult than she had expected.

She had scouted out several sheltered places she thought might do for sleeping, and was looking forward to a bit of stony privacy when Biddi said, "You did well, your first day. Tomorrow will be easier. This way."

"This way where?"

Janet, making a final inspection of the kitchens, said, "To bed, where do you think?"

"Up here." Biddi raised her candle and led the way. "Through the Great Hall and to the right. That's where the women's dormitory is. The men's dormitory is on the left."

"Is Janet coming?"

Nerissa's hope of a negative answer must have been obvious, for Biddi chuckled and said, "She's a privileged servant – she's been granted permission to marry. She and her husband have a little room on the next floor up."

As Biddi reached for the handle to the dormitory's door, Nerissa plucked at her sleeve. She had her alone. She could give her the old man's message. The razor, though, was Nerissa's prize and Nerissa's secret. If Biddi were supposed to be told about it, someone would have said so.

"What is it?" Biddi asked.

"It was you I was looking for."

"Me?"

Janet came up from the kitchen. She stopped when she saw Nerissa and Biddi.

"Dawdling, even to bed? You'd best get what sleep you can. The day starts early for the honest poor. Tell her that, Biddi, while you're talking."

"Good night, Janet," said the kitchen maid.

The cook still stood. So did Biddi, with Nerissa inching around behind her.

"I'm not losing my sleep over you," Janet said at last, and crossed the Hall to the stairwell.

When she was gone, Biddi whispered, "You were looking for me? Why?"

"I don't know why. An old man, bald, pulling a cart, told me to come looking for Biddi. He said to tell you the hen lays well."

"Andrin! You saw him…when?"

"This morning."

"Where?"

"On the road, between the bridge and here. He was coming from this direction."

"He was bald?"

Nerissa nodded.

"Pulling a cart?"

Nerissa nodded again. "What is it? It's something strange, isn't it?"

Biddi smiled and put a hand on the child's face. "Come into the dormitory. We'll find you a clean shift, and a pallet and a cover, and I'll tell you a story that happened about ten years ago…. Or maybe it was this morning."

Characters

(more or less in order of mention or appearance)

Darcy Aminta beren Valda (unmarried name: Darcy beren Aminta)	Roll-Keeper of Eastern District, then of Layounna. Husband of Devona, father of Elsie.
Devona beren Valda	Public scribe, wife of Darcy, mother of Elsie.
Elsie beren Devona	Chosen second wife of Landry.
Salvia Zglaria called Moder Zglaria	Old woman who lives in Fiddlewood.
Landry Oliva beren Ada (unmarried name: Landry beren Oliva)	Consort to Karol beren Ada.
Karol beren Ada	Kinninger (ruler) of Layounna. Chief of the House of Onagros. Wife of Landry.
Rhu beren Robia	Landry's Chamberlain.
Guthrie beren Melanell	Chief Sword under Landry.
Ada beren Cinnie	Mother of Karol beren Ada, Kinninger before her. Mother of Sorcha and Kinnan.
Gils Nara beren Ailith (unmarried name: Gils beren Nara)	Heart-husband and child-sire of Ada beren Cinnie and Osa beren Ailith, father of Cameron and Kinnan
Cameron beren Osa	Son of Gils Nara and Osa beren Ailith, half-brother to Kinnan, heart-husband and child-sire to Karol beren Ada
Kinnan beren Ada (birn Matka, beren Osa, beren Moder)	Son of Gils Nara and Ada beren Cinnie, half-brother to Karol, half-brother to Cameron. In line for throne of Layounna
Sorcha beren Ada	Karol beren Ada's younger sister, half-sister to Kinnan, wife of Hayward.

Oliva beren Audre	Thane of Sarpa. Mother of Landry, Hayward, and Corvina. An Adept of the dark Tarkastrian Arts.
Hayward Oliva beren Ada (unmarried name: Hayward beren Oliva)	Son of Oliva beren Audre, brother of Landry and Corvina, married to Sorcha.
Corvina beren Oliva	Daughter of Oliva, sister of Landry and Hayward. An alchemist specializing in poison.
Andrin beren Tooli	A Waymaster.
Biddi beren Anna	A kitchen maid, friends with Andrin.
Farukh Suria'Apa-Dan	A storyteller from the land of Sule.
Fala Salali	A trinket-woman from the land of Nishi.
Verrina beren Unna	Andrin's grandmother.
Chandler	A hen.
Trahern birn Lona	A blacksmith from the land of Kozabir.
Brady birn Ilka	Devona's apprentice from Kozabir.
Nerissa birn Matka	A slave.
Isa birn Isa and Barand Tara birn Isa	Nerissa's owners.
Audre beren Oda	Oliva beren Audre's mother. Thane of Oakwood.
Edelin beren Cinnie	Elsie's male disguise.
Vevay beren Sorcha Atwell beren Sorcha Joia beren Sorcha Blaine beren Sorcha	Children of Sorcha and Hayward.
Brina beren Moder	Waymistress of Kudasad Waystation.
Anshar "The Divine Spear" Redhand	A Layounnan rebel based in the land of Istok.
Janet beren Lana	Cook in the castle in Kudasad, capital of Layounna.
Bryan beren Basha	Captain of Landry's Swords.
Robeard Caitlin beren Regan	Thane of Leven. Spokesman of the Southern Council of Thanes.
Robia beren Dela	Rhu beren Robia's mother.

GENEALOGY

ONAGROS BEFORE INTERMARRIAGE

husband (unnamed)   +   Ada beren Cinnie   +   Gils Nara beren Ailith   +   Osa beren Ailith

Karol beren Ada   Sorcha beren Ada   Kinnan beren Ada (Osa. Moder)   Cameron beren Osa

No shared blood

SARPA BEFORE INTERMARRIAGE

Otemar Sadira beren Oliva   +   Oliva beren Oda

Landry beren Oliva   Hayward beren Oliva   Corvina beren Oliva

INTERMARRIAGE OF **ONAGROS** AND **SARPA**

Landry Oliva beren Ada   +   Karol beren Ada   +   Cameron beren Osa

?

Sorcha beren Ada   +   Hayward Oliva beren Ada

Vevay beren Sorcha   Atwell beren Sorcha   Joia beren Sorcha   Blaine beren Sorcha